VISIONS OF GERARD

Jack Kerouac

VISIONS OF GERARD

McGRAW-HILL BOOK COMPANY
New York   St. Louis   San Francisco   Düsseldorf   Mexico
Montreal   Panama   Paris   São Paulo   Tokyo   Toronto
Bogotá   Madrid

FIC

Reprinted by arrangement with Farrar, Straus & Giroux, Inc.

First McGraw-Hill Paperback edition, 1976

345678910 MUMU 898765432

Library of Congress Cataloging in Publication Data
Kerouac, John, 1922–1969.
     Visions of Gerard.

     Reprint of the 1963 ed. published by Farrar, Straus, New York.
     I. Title.
[PZ3.K4596Vi10]   [PS3521.E735]   813'.5'4   76-14217
ISBN 0-07-034204-0

VISIONS OF GERARD

Gerard Duluoz was born in 1917 a sickly little kid with a rheumatic heart and many other complications that made him ill for the most part of his life which ended in July 1926, when he was 9, and the nuns of St. Louis de France Parochial School were at his bedside to take down his dying words because they'd heard his astonishing revelations of heaven delivered in catechism class on no more encouragement than that it was his turn to speak——Saintly Gerard, his pure and tranquil face, the mournful look of him, the piteousness of his little soft shroud of hair falling down his brow and swept aside by the hand over blue serious eyes——I would deliver no more obloquies and curse at my damned earth, but obsecrations only, could I resolve in me to keep his fixed-in-memory face free of running off from me——For the first four years of my life, while he lived, I was not Ti Jean Duluoz, I was Gerard, the world was his face, the flower of his face, the pale stooped disposition, the heartbreakingness and the holiness and his teachings of tenderness to me, and my mother constantly reminding me to pay attention to his goodness and advice——Summers he'd lain a-afternoons, on back, in yard, hand to eyes, gazing at the white clouds passing on by, those perfect Tao phantoms that materialize and then travel and then go, dematerialized, in one vast planet emptiness, like souls of people, like substantial fleshy people

themselves, like your quite substantial redbrick smokestacks of the Lowell Mills along the river on sad red sun Sunday afternoons when big scowling Emil Pop Duluoz our father is in his shirtsleeves reading the funnies in the corner by the potted plant of time and home——Patting his sickly little Gerard on the head, *"Mon pauvre ti Loup,* me poor lil Wolf, you were born to suffer" (little dreaming how soon it would be his sufferings'd end, how soon the rain, incense and teary glooms of the funeral which would be held across the way in St.Louis de France's cellar-like basement church on Boisvert and West Sixth).

For me the first four years of my life are permeant and gray with the memory of a kindly serious face bending over me and being me and blessing me——The world a hatch of Duluoz Saintliness, and him the big chicken, Gerard, who warned me to be kind to little animals and took me by the hand on forgotten little walks.

"Allo zig lain——ziglain——zigluu——" he'd say to our cat, in a little high crazycatvoice and the cat'd look plain and blank back at him as though the cat language was the true one but also they understood the words to portend kindness and their eyes followed him as he moved around our gray house and suddenly they'd bless him unexpectedly by jumping on his lap at dusk, in the quiet hour when water's bur-

bling on the stove the starchy Irish potatoes and hushsilence fills ears in houses announcing Avalokitesvara's blessed everlasting presence grinning in the swarming shadows behind the stuffed chairs and tasseled lamps, a Womb of Exuberant Fertility the world and the sad things in it laughable, Gerard the least and last to dis-acknowledge it I'd bet if he were here to bless my pencil as I undertake and draw breath to tell his pain-tale for the world that needs his soft and loving like.

"Heaven is all white" (*le ciel yé tout blanc,* in the little child patois we spoke our native French in), "the angels are like lambs, and all the children and their parents are together forever," he'd tell me, and I: *"Sont-ils content?* Are they happy?"

"They couldnt be anything else but happy——"

"What's the color of God?——"

"Blanc d'or rouge noir pi toute——White of gold red black and everything——" is the translation.

Lil Kitty comes up and gricks wet nose and teethies against Gerard's outheld forefinger, "Whattayawant, *Ploo pli?"*——Would I could remember the huddling and the love of these forlorn two brothers in a past so distant from my sick aim now I couldnt gain its healing virtues if I had the bridge, having lost all my molecules of then without their taste of enlightenment.

He bundles me in the coat and hat, he'll show me how to play in the yard——Meanwhile smoke sorrows from red dusk roofs in winter New England and our shadows in the brown frozen grass are like remembrances of what must have happened a million aeons of aeons ago in the Same and blazing Nirvana-Samsara Blown-Out-Turned-On light.

KURT
1967-1994

I do believe I remember the gray morning (musta been a Saturday) when Gerard showed up at the cottage on Burnaby Street (when I was 3) with the little boy whose name I cant forget and the consistency of it like lumps of gray mud, Plourdes——Balls of sorrow are his name——Sniveling at the nose which he had no handkerchief to blow, dirty, in a little holey sweater, Gerard himself in his long black parochial stockings and the highbutton shoes, they're standing in the yard by the little wooden stoop in back of to the side where the meadows of sadness are faced (with their stand of gleary pines beyond and in which on rainy days I could see the beginning of the Indianface Fog)——Gerard wants Mama Ange to give the little boy Plourdes some bread and butter and bananas, *"Ya faim,* he's hungry"——From a poor and ignorant family, likely, and they'd never feed him except at supper, or an occasional (perhaps) lard sandwich, Gerard was acute enough to realize the child was hungry and was crying on account of hunger and he knew the munificence of his own mother's home and took him thereunto and asked for food for him——Which my mother gave the boy, who now, years later, I see, or just saw, on a recent visit to Lowell, six feet tall and 200 pounds and a lot of bread and butter and bananas and child largesse has gone into the

bulkying of his decaying mountain of flesh——A glimmer
memory maybe in his truckdriver brain of the tiny sickling
who mourned for him and fed him and blessed him in the
long ago——Plourdes——A Canadian name containing in it
for me all the despair, raw gricky hopelessness, cold and
chapped sorrow of Lowell——Like the abandoned howl of a
dog and no one to open the door——For Plourdes his fate,
for me:——Gerard to open it to the Love of God, whereby,
now, 30 years later, my heart, healed, is stillwarm, saved——
Without Gerard what would have happened to Ti Jean?

I'm on the porch muffled in bundlings watching the little
Christly drama——My mother goes in the kitchen and butters
bread and peels bananas, with that heartbreaking, slow,
fumbly motion of mothers of the world, like old Indian
Mothers who've pounded tortillas and boiled mush across
clanks of millenniums and wind-howl——My heart is where
it belongs.

My father comes home from work and hears the story and
says "How he's got a heart, that child!" shaking his head
and biting his lips by the stove.

It was only many years later when I met and understood
Savas Savakis that I recalled the definite and immortal
idealism which had been imparted me by my holy brother
——And even later with the discovery (or dullmouthed
amazed hang-middled mindburnt waking re discovery) of

Buddhism, Awakenedhood——Amazed recollection that from the very beginning I, whoever "I" or whatever "I" was, was destined, destined indeed, to meet, learn, understand Gerard and Savas and the Blessed Lord Buddha (and my Sweet Christ too through all his Paulian tangles and bloody crosses of heathen violence)——To awaken to pure faith in the bright one truth: All is Well, practice Kindness, Heaven is Nigh.

Gerard's sad eyes first foretold it——In the dream already ended, which all this is——His face so tranquil and compassionate, various pictures of him we had, one in particular in front of me now, that was taken in his (probably) fifth year, on the porch of the Lupine Road house the which, when I recently visited it, revealed to me (to my infant's old gaze) the ancient form of Earth-Beginnings in the form of a fluted porch-ceiling-light-globe that I had studied and studied with infant eyes long afternoons of drowse sun or warm March, in my crib——When, seeing it just recently, age 33, its contours rejoined me deeply with the long forgotten contours of Gerard's face and peculiar soft hair, and little Raskolnik parochial shirt, and high black stockings——Nay, and unto the very brown slats of the house next door, and even more nay-worse-so unto the very stone "castle" on top of the hill a field away which I had completely forgotten in my rational memory and saw with awe in maturity what already I'd divined unconsciously in teenage reveries of "Doctor Sax and the Castle of the Great World Snake" all to be explained ahead in the *Duluoz Legend*——The said

porch is the scene of the holy little snapshot here kept,
Gerard sitting on the rail with my sister Nin (then 3), holding her hand, smirky-ing in the sun the two of them as some
aunt or paternity godfather snaps the shot, the long forgotten snow of human hopes paling into browner stains in old
photoisms——I see there in the eyes of Gerard the very diamond kindness and patient humility of the Brotherhood
Ideal propounded from afar down the eternal corridors of
Buddhahood and Compassionate Sanctity, in Nirmana (appearance) Kaya (form)——My own brother, a spot of saint-
hood in the endless globular Universes and Chillicosm——His
heart under the little shirt as big as the sacred heart of thorns
and blood depicted in all the humble homes of French-
Canadian Lowell.

Behold: — One day he found a mouse caught in Scoop's
mousetrap outside the fish market on West Sixth Street——
Faces more bleak than envenomed spiders, those who invented mousetraps, and had paths of bullgrained dullishness
beaten to their bloodstained doors, and crowed in the sill——
For that matter, on this gray morning, I can remember the
faces of the Canucks of Lowell, the small tradesmen,
butchers, butter and egg men, fishmen, barrelmakers, bums
in benches (no benches but the oldtime sidewalk chair
spitters by the dump, by banana peels steaming in the midday broil)——The hungjawed dull faces of grown adults who

had no words to praise or please little trying-angels like
Gerard working to save the mouse from the trap——But just
stared or gawped on jawpipes and were silly in their prime
——The little mouse, thrashing in the concrete, was released
by Gerard——It went wobbling to the gutter with the fish-
juice and spit, to die——He picked it tenderly and in his
pocket sowed the goodness——Took it home and nursed it,
actually bandaged it, held it, stroked it, prepared a little basket for it, as Ma watched amazed and men walked around in
the streets "doin good for themselves" rounding up paper
beyond their beans——Bums! all!——A thought smaller
than a mouse's turd directed to the Sunday Service Mass
necessity, and that usually tinged by inner countings how
much they'll plap in th'basket——I dont remember ration-
ally but in my soul and mind Yes there's a mouse, peeping,
and Gerard, and the basket, and the kitchen the scene of this
heart-tender little hospital——"That big thing hurt you
when it fell on your little leg" (because Gerard could really
feel empathetically that pain, pain he'd had enough to not
be apprentice at the trade and pang)——He could feel the
iron snap grinding his little imagined birdy bones and
squeezing and cracking and pressing harder unto worse-
than-death the bleak-in-life——For it's not innocent blank
nature made hills look sad and woe-y, it's men, with their
awful minds——Their ignorance, grossness, mean petty
thwarthings, schemes, hypocrite tendencies, repenting over
losses, gloating over gains——Pot-boys, bone-carriers, funeral
directors, glove-wearers, fog-breathers, shit-betiders, pissers,

befoulers, stenchers, fat calf converters, utter blots & scabs on
the face of it the earth——"Mouse? Who cares about a gad
dam mouse——God musta made em to fit our traps"——
Typical thought—I'd as soon drop a barrel of you-know-
what on the roof of my own house, as walk a mile in
conversation about one of them—I dont count Gerard in
that seedy lot, that crew of bulls——The particular bleak
gray jowled pale eyed sneaky fearful French Canadian
quality of man, with his black store, his bags of produce, his
bottomless mean and secret cellar, his herrings in a barrel,
his hidden gold rings, his wife and daughter jongling in
another dumb room, his dirty broom in the corner, his
piousness, his cold hands, his hot bowels, his well-used whip,
his easy greeting and hard opinion——Lay me down in sweet
India or old Tahiti, I dont want to be buried in *their* cemetery——In fact, cremate me and deliver me to *les Indes,* I'm
through——Wait till I get going on some of these other blood-
louts, for that matter——Yet not likely Gerard ever, if he'd
have lived, would have fattened as I to come and groan about
peoples and in plain print loud and foolish, but was a soft
tenderhearted angel the likes of which you'll never find
again in science fictions of the future with their bleeding
plastic penis-rods and round hole-machines and worries
about how to get from Pit to Pisspot which is one millionth
of a billionth of an inch further in endlessness of our gracious
Lord than the earth speck (which I'd spew) (if I were you)
(Maha Meru)——Some afternoon, Gerard goes to school
——It had been on a noontime errand when sent to the store

to buy smoked fish, that he'd found the mouse—Now, smiling, I see him from my overstuffed glooms in the parlor corner walking up Beaulieu Street to school with his strapped books and long black stockings and that peculiar gloomy sweetness of his person that was all things to me, I saw nothing else——Happy because his mouse was fed and repaired and safe in her little basket——Innocent enough comes our cat in the mid drowses of day, and eats, and leaves but the tail, enough to make all Lowell Laugh, but when Gerard comes home at 4 to see his tail-let in the bottom of the poor little basket he'd so laboriously contrived, he cried ——I cried too.

My mother tried to explain that it wasnt the cat's fault and nobody's fault and such was life.

He knew it wasn't the cat's fault but he took Nanny and sat her on the rocking chair and held her jowls and delivered her an exhortation no less:

"*Méchante!* Bad girl! Dont you understand what you've done? When will you understand? We dont disturb little animals and little things! We leave them alone! We'll never go to heaven if we go on eating each other and destroying each other like that all the time!——without thinking, without knowing!——wake up, foolish girl!——realize what you've done!——Be ashamed! shame! crazy face! stop wiggling your ears! Understand what I'm tellin you! It's got to stop some fine day! There wont always be time! ——Bad girl! Go on! Go in your corner! Think it over well!"

I had never seen Gerard angry.

I was amazed and scared in the corner, as one might have felt seeing Christ in the temple bashing the moneychanger tables everywhichaway and scourging them with his seldom whip.

When my father comes home from his printing shop and undoes his tie and removes 1920's vest and sits himself down at hamburger and boiled potatoes and bread and butter of the prime with the kiddies and the good wife, the proposition is put up to him why men be so cruel and mice betrayed and cats devour the rest——Why we were made to suffer and be harsh in return, one the other, and drop turds of iron on brows of hope, and mop up sick yards and sad—— "I'll tell you, Ti Gerard, little one, in life it's a jungle, man eats man either you eat or get eaten——The cat eats the mouse, the mouse eats the worm, the worm eats the cheese, the cheese turns and eats the man——So to speak——It's like that, life——Dont cry and dont bother your sweet lil head over these things——All right, we're all born to die, it's the same story for everybody, see? We eat the cow and the cow gives us milk, dont ask me why."

"Yes, why——why do men make traps for little mice?"

"Because they eat their grain."

"Their old grain."

"It's grain that's in our bread——Look here, you eat it your bread? I dont see you throw it on the floor! and you dont make *passes* with the dust in the corner!"——*Passes* were the name Gerard had invented for when you run your bread over gravy, my mother'd do the soaking and throw the *passes* all around the table, even to me in my miffles and bibs at the little child flaptable——But because of our semi-Iroquoian French-Canadian accent *passe* was pronounced *PAUSS* so I can still hear the lugubrious sound of it and comfort-a-suppers of it, *M'ué'n pauss,* as you'd expect Bardolph to remember his cockwalloping heigho's of Eastcheap ——My father is in the kitchen, young and primey, shirtsleeves, chomping up his supper, grease on his chin, bemused, explaining moralities to his angels——They'll grow 12 feet tall in the grave ere the monstrance that contains the solution to the problem be held up to shine and make true belief to shine, there's no explaining your way out of the evil of existence——"In any case, eat or be eaten——We eat now, later on the worms eat us."

Truer words were not spoken from any vantage point on this packet of earth.

"Why? *Pourquoi?*" cries lil Gerard with his brows forming woe and inabilities——"I dont want it to be like this, me."

"Though you want or not, it is."

"I dont care."

"What you gonna do?"

He pouts; he'll go to heaven, that's what; enough of this beastliness and compromising gluttony and compensating muck——Life, another word for mud.

"Come, come, little Gerard, maybe there's something you know that *we* dont know"——My father always did concede, Gerard had a deep mind and deep things to think that didnt find nook in insurance policies and printer's bills——They'd never write Gerard a policy but in eternity, he knew we were here a short while, and pathetic like the mouse, and O patheticker like the cat, and O worse! like the father-cant-explain!

"Awright," he'll go to bed and sleep it off, he'll tuck me in too, and kiss Ti Nin goodnight and the mouse be no lesser for her moment in his hands at noon——Together we pray for the Mouse. "Dear Lord, take care of the little mouse"——"Take care of the cat," we add to pray, since that's where the Lord'll have to do his work.

Ah, and the winds are cold and blow forlorner dust than they'll ever be able to invent in hell, in Northern Earth here, where people's hopes though warm fail to conceal the draft, the little draft that works all night moving curtains over radiator heat and sneaks around your blanket, and would bring you outdoors where russet dawn-men with cold-chapped ham-hands saw and pound at wood and work and steam with horses and curse the Satan in the air that made all Russias, Siberias, Americas bare to the blasts of infinity.

Gerard and I huddle in the warm gleeful bed of morning, afraid to get out——It's like remembering before you were born and your hap was at hand and Karma forced you out to start the story.

"Where is she the little mouse now?"

"This morning. The cat has shat her in the woods (*Le chat l'a shiez dans l'champ*)——with the little pipi yellow you see in the snow down there, see it?"

"*Oui.*"

"*Voilà* your fly of last summer, she's dead too——"

We think it over in motionless trance, as Ma prepares Pa's breakfast in the fragrant kitchen below.

"Angie," says Dad at the stove, "that kid'll break my heart yet——it hurt him so much to lose his little mouse."

"He's all heart."

"With his sickness inside——Ah, it busts my head—— Eat or get eaten——not men?——Hah!——There's a gang downtown would, if their guts were big enough."

Gerard's feeling of the holiness of life extended into the realm of romance.

A drunkard under an ample tent was never more adamant

concerning how his little sister should behave——"Mama, look what Ti Nin's doing she's going to school with her overshoes flopping and throwing her behind around like a flapper!" he yelled one morning looking out the window——It was one of those days when he was suffering a rheumatic fever relapse and had to stay in bed, weeks sometimes, some days worse than others——"Aw look at her!——" He was horrified——He refused to let her do it, when she came home at noon he had a speech worked out for her——"I'm telling you Gerard, you'll be a priest some day!" my mother'd say.

Meanwhile the kids at church did the sign of the cross some of them with the following words:

"Au nom du père
Ma tante Cafière
Pistalette de bois
Ainsi soit-il"

Meaning

"In the name of the Father
My Aunt Cafière
Pistolet of wood
Amen"

There's my pa——Emil Alcide Duluoz, at that time, 1925 a hale young printer of 36, dark complexioned, frowning, serious, hardjawed but soft in the gut (tho he had a gut so

hard when he oomfed it and dared us kids butt our heads
in it or punch fists off it and it felt like punching a powerful
basketball)——5:7, Bretonsquat, blue eyed——He had a
habit I cant forget, even now I just imitated it, lighting a
small fire in the ashtray, out of cigarette pack paper or
tobacco wrapping——Sitting in his chair he'd watch the
little Nirvana fire consume the paper and render it black
crisp void, and understand, mayhap, the bigger kindling of
the 3,000 Chillicosms——That which would devour and di-
gest to safety——A little matter of time, for him, for me,
for you.

Too, he'd take fresh crisp MacIntosh apples of the Fall
and sit in his easy chair and peel em with his pocket knife,
making long tassels around and around the fruitglobe so
perfect you could have hung them like tassels' canopies
from chandelier to chandelier in the Hall Tolstoy, the
which we'd take and sling around and I'd eat em in like
great tapeworms and they'd end up flung out in the garbage
can like coils of electric wire around and around——After
which he'd eat his peeled apple at the gisty whitemeat cut-
surface with great slobbering juicy bites that had all the
world watering——"Imitate the roar of a lion! Imitate a
tiger cat! Imitate an elephant!"——Which he'd do, in his
chair, for us, evenings in New England, Gerard on one knee,
me on the other, Nin on his lap——That is, when ever there
was no poker game to speak of downtown.

"And you my little Gerard, why do you look so pensive
tonight? What's goin on in that little head?" he'd say, hug-

ging his Gerard to him, cheek against soft hair, as Nin and
I watched rave lip't and rapt in the happiness of our child-
hood, little dreaming what quick work the winds of outside winter would do against the timbers and tendons of
his poor house.

In the name of the father, the son, and the Holy Ghost,
amen.

Gerard had birds that neighbor and relative could swear
did know him personally, they came to his windowsill
in the time of his long illnesses, especially Spring, when
his rheum-rimmed eyes'd look out on fresh undefiled mornings like captured princesses in must towers——Vile visitations of bile'd turned him green, and white, in the night, his
bedpan beneath the bed, but for the birds he had roses for
words——*"Arrive, mes ti's anges,* Come my little Angels,"
and he'd sow his (by Ma prepared) breadcrumbs on the sill
and on the short slope roof up there where his sickroom was
(a location for a room that forever frets my brain when in
gray dreams I dream of houses, that location is always the
one that makes me sink, somewhere to the north and west
of misery, by peaks, mystery, gables)——Cherry blossom'd
May brought him hundreds of gay birds with gloomy beaks
that chattered on the roof around his crumbs——But he'd
cry: "Why dont the little birds come to me?! Dont they
know I wont hurt them?"

"Of course they dont, they cant know——for all they know you're a boy, and boys hurt birds."

"And birds hurt boys?"

"And birds never hurt a boy, but the boy will stone his dozen and upset the nests of a dozen fledgelings in his nasty prime."

"Why? Why is everyone so mean? Didnt God see to it that we——of all people——*people*——would be kind——to each other, to animals."

God made no provisions for that winter.

The birds chatter, come come close at hand, he glees and jumps up and down at his pillow: "That one's coming, that one I'm tellin you, he'll end up in my hand!"

"I hope," my mother'd say with wise eyes and unwisely in the night pray for it and worthily praise him——My father couldnt believe it.

"Ah, if I could buy him birds!"

"Just one little bird, just ONE," he'd cry, as I sat in my little chair by the bed watching, fingering the crumb pan with little pudgy fingers so fat they called me *Ti Pousse*, Little Thumb.

"Come here, Little Thumb, look, the little grey bird, doesnt he look like he wants to eat in my hand and give me a little kiss?"

"Yes."

"Wouldnt you like to kiss that little thing?"

"Yes."

"Yes yes little bird come on."

But a chance noise of breadtruck drives the whole flock away *kavroom,* for the next tree, where they jabber the new news——Tears come to Gerard's eyes, his lips form a fateful pout, a groan comes, it means "Ah what's the use——if I loved them any more they'd have honey and balm for breakfast and have beaks of gold, yet they avoid me like a rat dripping bacteria——like a falcon——like a man."

"Gerard," my mother'd explain, "dont make yourself sad about the little birds. Do you know why? Because God sees and knows you love them and he'll reward you."

"In heaven I'll have all the birds I want."

"Yes in heaven——and maybe on earth, have courage, patience."

With his little belly he heaves a heigh ho sigh, 't'would be a good thing to be in that snowy somewhere and rosy nowhere where patience is just a word and no bellies burdenly pain. "Yes, in heaven there are birds, millions of birds, even smaller than these, big like butterflies, smaller, like ants, white like an angel——everywhere." He'd turn to his drawing board propped on his lap and start drawing his dreary eternities and dreams of paradise. He was an amazing artist at the age of 8. He drew pictures that my old man actually disbelieved as his own when he saw them a-nights:

"Gerard did that?——look here!"

Ditto my father's friends——To prove it he'd draw right in front of them, boats sailing on the blue ocean (copied from the Saturday Evening Post), birds, bridges, lambies, people's hats——Also he had an erector set and built up

impossible engineering marvels like vast complicated ferris wheels and race cars and the usual tote-cranes and trucks that were borrowed from the book of instructions——Heaving the book aside he'd of a sick morning (as I watch) whip up beautiful little baby carriages or baby cribs for Nin to put her dolls in at noon, all set with little draperies——I wonder if she still remembers these latter days as she stares at Television's rancid blight whole evenings in her home parlor, waiting to join him in Heaven——

For me he'd concoct delights at the drop of my saying it, "Make me a *ritontu,*" which is I dont know what, and he'd make a crazy construction and I'd play with it and try to unscrew it and chew the edges of it——

Then the birds would come flocking and singin in rollicking nations around our holy roof again, and he'd call for bread, and multiply it in crumbs, and sow it to the sisters who pecked and picked——

"*Vien, vien, vien,*" the picture of him hand outstretched and helpless in bed calling at the open window for the celestial visitors, enough to make my heart leap from a cold indifferent lair (of late)——

He never got his hand on a bird, naturally, and what transformation might have taken place in such a case I do not know——

Meanwhile Dr. Simpkins came and went with his oldfashioned satchel and his listen-tubes and pipes and pills and pumps and surprised us all by his gravity and inability to speak——He had no long hope for the iife of Gerard.

I didnt understand anything that was going on, I was rosy plump Little Thumb *Ti Pousse* glad to be in the same world as Gerard.

One night we're on the kitchen floor with the Boston American, I remember distinctly the pinksheet Hearst evening news, on the front page is the photo of a woman who's murdered someone, I take my scissors and stab her right in the eye impaling the paper on the linoleum ——"*Non non Ti Jean* never do that!" Didnt understand (as I remember myself) the glee, the mindless happy glee that went into that vigorous stab——But to Gerard the mindlessness was precisely the horror and the currency of a hateful hopeless world——"*Non, non,* never do anything like that, ——Ah poor Ti Pousse, you dont understand——Look, take out the scissors, fix her eyes"——We smooth the ruffled paper, stroke the paper lady's eyes, brood over our sin, rectify hells, fruition good Karmas for ourselves, repent, go to confession——His lips tsk tsk and pout——Kissable Gerard, to kiss him and that pout of pain must have been as soft a sin as kissing a lamb in the belly or an angel in her wing—— He gave me piggybacks to prove that other pastimes were better and that I was forgiven——He even let me "beat him up" in mock fights where we rolled on the linoleum and I screamed——

With my little hands clasped behind me I stand at the

kitchen window, sometime not long after, on a gray blizzard day, watching the inky snowflakes descend from infinity and hit the ground where they become miraculous white, whereby I understand why Gerard was so white and because of man came of such black sources——It was by virtue of his pain-on-earth, that his black was turned to white.

It's a cold crisp morning in October, Gerard is going to school with his books and bread and butter and banana lunch and an apple——I watch him going down Beaulieu Street, alone——Gangs of kids run around——At the end of Beaulieu Street is the large gravel play yard of the Green Public School where because the kids werent Catholics the nuns have been telling Gerard and Nin and the kids of St. Louis de France Parochial School that they have tails concealed beneath their trousers——Which some of us (I for one) seriously believe——At that street Gerard turns right to go to St. Louis which is right there along three wooden fences of bungalows, first you see the nun's home, redbrick and bright in the morning sun, then the gloomy edifice of the schoolhouse itself with its longplank sorrow-halls and vast basement of urinals and echo calls and beyond the yard, with its special (I never forgot) little inner yard of cinder gravel separated from the big dirt yard (which becomes a field down at Farmer Kenny's meadow) by a small granite wall not a foot high, that everyone sits on or throw cards against——The big game is card slinging, the bubblegum cards with pictures of movie stars and base-ball players (Great God! it musta been Vilma Banky and Rogers Hornsby with young faces on the fragrant bubble-gum cards)——They are flung against the wall, nearest wins ——The big game at recess——Gerard comes slowly rumi-nating in the bright morn among the happy children—— Today his mind is perplexed and he looks up into the per-fect cloudless empty blue and wonders what all the bruiting and furor is below, what all the yelling, the buildings, the humanity, the concern——"Maybe there's nothing at all," he divines in his lucid pureness——"Just like the smoke that comes out of Papa's pipe"——"The pictures that the smoke makes"——"All I gotta do is close my eyes and it all goes away"——"There *is* no Mama, no Ti Jean, no Ti Nin, Papa ——no me——no *kitigi*" (the cat)——"There is no earth—— look at the perfect sky, it says nothing"——Little snively Plourdes is losing at a game of cards in the corner, the bullies buffet him out——"He's crying——he only thinks of his luck and his luck is worse"——"his luck is mixed up in the bad and the poor"——"Ah the world"——To the other end is the *Presbytère* (Rectory) where Father Pere La-lumière the *Curé* lives, and other priests, a yellow brick house awesome to the children as it is a kind of chalice in itself and we imagine candle parades in there at night and snow white lace at breakfast——Then the church, St. Louis de France, a basement affair then, with concrete cross, and inside the ancient smooth pews and stained windows and stations of the cross and altar and special altars for Mary and Joseph and antique mahogany confessionals with winey drapes and ornate peep doors——And vast solemn marble basins in which the old holy water lies, dipped by a thousand hands——And secret alcoves, and upper organs, and sacrosanct backrooms where altar boys emerge in lace and blacks and the priests march forth bearing kingly ornaments—— Where Gerard had been and kept on going many a time, he liked to go to church——It was where God had his due ——"When I get to Heaven the first thing I'm gonna ask God is for a beautiful little white lamb to pull my wagon ——*Ai,* I'd like to be there right away already, not have to wait——" He sighs among the birds and kids, and over at the end of the yard are gathered the teacher nuns getting ready for the morning bell and lineup, the morning breeze moving their black robes and pendant black rosaries slightly, their faces pale around rheumy eyes, delicate as lacework their features, distant as chalices, rare as snow, untouchable as holy bread of the host, the mothers of thought——Striking awe in children——Monastic ladies devoted to sewing and devout service in their gloomy redbrick hermitage there where we saw them in the windows with their cap flares and cameo profiles bent over rosaries or missals or embroideries, they themselves mostly all the time vigorously curiously digging the scene outdoors——In fact right now a hobo from Louisiana and the East Texas Oil fields who happens to be passing thru Lowell, lies in the straw grass below the Green School fence, knee on knee, grass in mouth, contemplating the flawless void and humming the blues and what could be the thoughts of the old nun at the window watching him——"Lazy bum! (*Paresseux!*)"——"Robber! ——Sinner!"

Typical of Gerard that he doesnt look to the fields, the trees down further where Farmer Kenny's fields become a thicket and after a few cottages of Centerville spurting morning smoke the distant hills and horizon meadows of on-to-Dracut and New Hampshire and all that pale brown promise of the sere continent——Gerard was inward turned like a chalice of gold bearing a single holy host, bounden to his glory doom——He sits on the little wall contemplating the kids, and the bum in the field, the nuns in the window, the little girls hopskotching beyond and where Ti Nin is screaming with the rest——"Little crazy, look at her gettin all excited——she doesnt understand the blue sky this morning, she doesnt care like a little kitty——But look ——" he looks up, mouth agape——"There's nothing there, not a cloud, not a sound——just like it was water upside-down and what's the bugs down here?" The air is crisp and good, he breathes it in——The bell rings and all the scufflers go to shuffle in the dreary lines of class by class with the head nun overlooking all, the parade ground formation of the new day, latecomers running thru the yard with flying books——A dog barking, and the coughs, and the gritty gravel under restless many little shoes——Another day of school——But Gerard has eyes up to sky and knows he'll never learn in school what he'd like to learn this morn-

ing from that sky of silent mystery, that heartbreaking sayless blank that wont tell men and boys what's up——
"It's the eye of God, there's no bottom——"
"Gerard Duluoz, you're not in line——!"
"Yes, Sister Marie."
"Silence! The Mother *Supérieure* is going to talk!"
"Ssst! Mercier! Give me my card!"
"It's mine!"
"It is not!"
"Shut your trap! (*Famme ta guêle*)."
"I'll fix you."
"P r r r r t"
"Silence!"

Silence over all, the rustle of the wind, the banners of two hundred hearts are still——Under that liquid everpresent impossible-to-understand undefiled blue——

A few Fall trees reach faint red twigs to it, smoke-smells wraith to twist like ghosts in noses of morning, the saw of Boisvert Lumberyard is heard to whine at a log and whop it, the rumble of the junkmen's cart on Beaulieu Street, one little kid cry far off——Souls, souls, the sky receives it all——Nobody can comment on the only reality which is Crystal Naught not even Viking Press——Not even Père Lalumière who now with clothesline-fresh garments parades downhall in the *Presbytère* whistling to his room, *lacrimae rerum* of the world in his smarting morning eyes, pettling and purtling with his lips at thought of the good *cortons* porkscraps for breakfast comin up just now soon's he gets his dud-o's on and sweeps officially to another day as *Curé* of the World——A good man and true, like Our Mayor in his City Hall and the President Coolidge at his desk 500 miles South to the morning that brights the Potomac same as brights the Merrimac of Lowell——In other words, and who will be the human being who will ever be able to deliver the world from its idea of itself that it actually exists in this crystal ball of mind?——One meek little Gerard with his childly ponderings shall certainly come closer than Caesarian bust-provokers with quills and signatures and cabinets and vestal dreary laceries——I say.

O, to be there on that morning, and actually see my Gerard waiting in line with all the other little black pants and the little girls in their own lines all in black dresses trimmed with white collars, the cuteness and sweetness and dearness of that oldfashion'd scene, the poor complaining nuns doing what they think is best, within the Church, all within Her Folding Wing——Dove's the church——I'll never malign that church that gave Gerard a blessed baptism, nor the hand that waved over his grave and officially dedicated it ——Dedicated it back to what it is, bright celestial snow not mud——Proved him what he is, ethereal angel not Festerer ——The nuns had a habit of whacking the kids on the knuckles with the edge part of the ruler when they didnt remember 6 × 7, and there were tears and cries and calamities in every classroom every day——And all the usual—— But it was all secondary, it was all for the bosom of the

Grave Church, which we all know was Pure Gold, Pure
Light.

That bright understanding that lights up the mind of
the soldier who decides to fight to death——"O Arjuna,
fight!"——That's what's implied at the rail of the altar
of repentance, for the repenter gives up self and admits
he was a fool and can only be a fool and may his bones
dissolve in the light of forever——*All* my sins, leaving not
jot or tittle out, even unto the smallest least-noticeable al-
most-not-sin that you could have got away with with another
interpretation——But you humbling fool you're a mass of
sin, a veritable barrel of it, you swish and swash in it like
molasses——You ooze mistakes thru your frail crevasses——
You've bungled every opportunity to bless somebody's brow
——You had the time, you will have the time, you'll yawn
and wont understand——Ah you're a bum as you are——
'T were better to dissolve you——The Holy Milk you act
like a curdler and a bacteria in it, yellow scum, sometimes
purple or pot green——As you are, it wont do——The Lord
knows he made a mistake——We talk about "the Lord"
out of the corner of our hands for want of a better way to
describe the undefilable emptiness of the blue sky on such
mornings as the morning Gerard wondered——It's typical
of us to compromise and anthropomorphalize and He it,
thus attributing to that bright perfection of Heaven our own

low state of selfbeing and selfhood and selfconsciousness
and selfness general——The Lord is no-*body*——The Lord
is no bandyer with forms——All conditional and talk, what
I have to say, to point it out——Miserable as a dull sermon
on a dull rainy morning in a damp church in the North,
and Sunday to boot——We are baptized in water for no un-
sanitary reason, that is to say, a well-needed *bath* is implied
——Praise a woman's legs, her golden thighs only produce
black nights of death, face it——Sin is sin and there's no
erasing it——We are spiders. We sting one another.

No man exempt from sin any more than he can avoid a
trip to the toilet.

Gerard and all the boys did special novenas at certain
seasons and went to confession on Friday afternoon, to prepare for Sunday morning when the church hoped to infuse
them with some of the perfection embodied and implied in
the concept of Christ the Lord——Even Gerard was a sinner.

I can see him entering the church at 4 P M, later than
the others due to some errand and circumstance, most of
the other boys are thru and leaving the church with that
lightfooted way indicative of the weight taken off their
minds and left in the confessional——The redemption
gained at the altar rail with penalty prayers, doled out
according to their lights and darknesses——Gerard doffs his
cap, trails fingertip in the font, does the sign of the cross
absently, walks half-tiptoe around to the side aisle and down
under the crucified tablets that always wrenched at his heart
when he saw them ("*Pauvre Jésus,* Poor Jesus") as tho Jesus

had been his close friend and brother done wrong indeed——
He genuflects and enters the pew and puts little knees to
plank, the plank is worn and dusted with a million kneeings
morning noon and night——He starts a preliminary prayer
——"Hail Mary——" in French the prayer: *"Je vous salue
Marie pleine de grâce"*——Grace and grease interlardedly
mixed, since the kids didnt say "grace," they said "grawse"
and no power on earth could stop them——The Holy Grease,
and good enough——*"Le Seigneur est avec vous——vous êtes
bénie entre toutes les femmes"*——Blessed among and above
all women, and they saw their mother's and sister's eyes
as one pair of eyes—*"Et Jésus le fruit de vos entrailles"*——
"entrailles" the powerful French word for Womb, *entrails,*
none of us had any idea what it meant, some strange interior
secret of Mary and Womanhood, little dreaming the whole
universe was one great Womb——The coil of that thought
and wording, not conducive to a true understanding of the
nature and emptiness-aspect of Wombhood, the perfect blue
sky's our Womb (but not our guts and coils)——*"Sainte
Marie, Mère de Dieu, priez pour nous, pécheurs, maintenant
et à l'heure de notre mort"*——No comma in the minds and
thoughts of the little boys (and their fathers) who ran it
straight thru *"pécheurs maintenant et à l'heure de notre
mort"*, sinner always right unto death, no help no hope,
born——

"Ainsi soit-il," amen, none of them knowing either what
that meant, "thus it is," it is what is and that's all it is——
thinking *ainsi soit-il* to be some mystic priestly secret word

invoked at altar——The innocence and yet intrinsic purity-understanding with which the Hail Mary was done, as Gerard, now knelt in his secure pew, prepares to visit the priest in his ambuscade and palace hut with the drapes that keep swishing aside as repentent in-and-out sinners come-and-go burdened and disemburdened as the case may be and is, amen——

Now Gerard ponders his sins, the candles flicker and testify to it——Dogs burlying in the distance fields sound like casual voices in the waxy smoke nave, making Gerard turn to see——But in and throughout all a giant silence reigns, 'shhhhhing, throughout the church like loud remindful ever-continuing abjuration to stay be straight and honest with your thought——

"I pushed lil Carrufel"——It took place in the schoolyard, with throw-cards Gerard had contrived a card-castle at midday recess, the first grader knocked it down coming too close and curious, without reflection Gerard raged and pushed him, really mad, "Look what you done to my house——Nut!" then instantly repented and too late——Now he pouts to concede: "But it was my house——*mautadit fou*" (a form of dyazam fool, or, drazyam, or whichever, used by children and in fact everyone including prelates, congressmen and druggists)——"But when I pushed him he turned pale, he didn't know anybody was gonna push him at that moment and that was the moment that hurt him——*Ya venu blême comme une vesse de carême* (He got pale as a lenten fart) ——His heart sank, and it's *me* that done it——It's a clear sin——My Jesus wouldnt have liked that watching from his cross"——He turns eyes up and around to the cross, where, with arms extended and hands nailed, Jesus sags to his footrest and bemoans the scene forever, and always it strikes in Gerard's naturally pitiful heart the thought "But *why* did they do that?"——Looking there at the foolish mistakes of past multitudes, plain as day to see, right on the wall—— The massive silence enveloping the graceful gentle form of hip and loincloth, limbs and knees, and the tortured thin breast——And the unforgettable downcast face——"God said to his son, we've got to do this——they decided in Heaven——and they did it——it happened——INRI!"—— "INRI——that means, it happened!——or else, INRI, the funny ribbon on the cross of the lover they killed——and, they put a nail through it"——Whatever mysterious thoughts that lie beneath in the bent heads of people and children in churches and temples century after century——"He's crying!" moaned Gerard, seeing it all.

Two other sins to confess: the deep sin of looking at Lajoie's and Lajoie could look at his, at the urinals, Wednesday morning, in the corner, for a long time——On purpose ——Gerard blushes to think of it——He sees the strange image of Lajoie's, different, curlier than his, he twinges to urinate namelessly and twists in his knee rest with the horror of his shame, not knowing——Sin's so deeply ingrained in us we invent them where they aint and ignore them where they are——Across his mind sneaks the proposition to avoid referring to the priest——But God will know

——And to mock the kindly ear of the listener Priest, who expects what there is, by removing one whit, a human sin divine to discover——"Poor Father Priest, what'll he know if I dont tell him? he wont know anything and he'll comfort me and send me off with my prayer, well it'll be a big sin to hide him a sin——like if I'd spit in his eyes when he's dead, like"——

The fortunate priest, Père Anselme Fournier, of Trois Rivières Quebec, the last of twelve sons but the first in his father's eye, pink-handed where he might have been horny-handed from the soil of Abraham, receives Ti Gerard in the confessional by sliding open his panel and bending quick ear obedient and loaded with long afternoon——Coughs revolve around the ceiling and sail and set in the pew sea, a knee-rest scrapes Sca-ra-at! with a harsh harmonizing *bang* from the altar where a worker creaks around with chair and candle snuffer——

"Bénit" is the only word, "bless," Gerard hears as the priest quickly mutters the introductory invocation and then his ear is ready——Gerard can faintly smell the adult breath and that peculiar adult smell of old teeth in old mouths long at work——"Bz bz bz" he hears as his predecessor in the confessional, just let out, prays fast and furious his repentant penalty rosaries at the rear seat half on his way to run out and slap cap on and run screaming across dusk stained fields of stubble and raw mud, to gangs in clover dales wrangling with rocks——A bird zings across the reddening late sky and over the roof of St. Louis de

France, as though the Holy Ghost wanted it——Saffron is the east, white is the west, where a bank cloud hides the thrower Sun, but soon it'll all girdle and engolden and be rich red gambling sunset splendor, again, as yesterday—— No school tomorrow is the frost announcement in the field grass, in the quiet corners of the schoolyards——Gerard senses all this but his day's work is just begun.

"My father, I confess that I pushed a little boy because he made me mad."

"Did you hurt him?"

"No——but I hurt his heart."

The priest is amazed to hear the refinement of it, the hairsplitting elegant point of it, ("He'll make a priest" he inner grins).

"Yes, you're right, my child, it hurt his heart. *Why* did you push him?" he pursues in conclusion with that sorrowful tender sorriness of the priest in the confessional as tho and as much to say "When all is said and done, why do we sit here and have to admit the sinningness of man."

"I pushed him because he had broken my little cardhouse."

"Ah."

"It made me mad."

"You flew into a rage."

"*Oui.*"

"You didnt think——He was younger than you."

"*Oui,* just a little boy of the first grade."

"Aw,"——regretfully the fine priest looks around at

Gerard briefly, commisserating as tender heart to tender heart——Ah, a scene going on in the little church of dusk! And somewhere wars!

"Well," to conclude, "you know your sin——You'll have to keep your patience the next time——Keep well your idea, that you hurt his heart if not his body"——admiringly—— "you've understood it yourself. I am certain," he takes trouble to add in spite of an overburdened afternoon of work in there, "that the Lord understands you.——And, there is something else you want to tell me."

"Yes my father"——and this Gerard says feeling like a beast piling animality on animality,——"I——er——" he stammers, confuses, and blushes, and stops.

"I'm waiting, my little boy."

Quickly Gerard whispers him the news about the urinal, Saturday Afternoon Confessions in St. All's had never heard a lurider admission it would seem from the stealth of his ps-ps'es.

"Ah, and did you touch his little dingdong?" (*Sa tite gidigne*).

Gerard: "*Aw non!*" glad he has a loophole and all because he never thought of it, mayhap——

"Well," sighing, "I have confidence in you my child that you'll never do it again. And something else? anything else?"

Gerard instantly remembers still another sin, forgotten until then——"I told the Sister I had studied my Catechism, and no I hadnt studied it."

"And you didnt know it?"

"Yes I knew it, but from another time, I remembered."

("Ah, that's no sin," thinks the Priest) and closes up accounts with: "Very well, that's all? Well then, say your rosary and fifteen Hail Mary's."

"Yes my father."

The gracious slide door slides, Gerard is facing the good happy wood, he runs out and hurries lightfoot to the altar, fit to sing——

It's all over! It was nothing! He's pure again!

He prays and bathes in prayers of gratitude at the white rail near the blood red carpet that runs to the stainless altar of white-and-gold, he clasps little hands over leaned elbows with hallelujahs in his eyes——To be God, and to've seen his eyes, looking up at my altar, with that beholding bliss, all because of some easy remission of mine, were hells of guilt I'd say——But God is merciful and God above all is kind, and kind is kind, and kindness is all, and it all works out that the mortal angel at the altar rail as the church hour roars with empty silence (everybody gone now, including the last priest, Gerard's priest) is bathed in blisskindness whether it would be pointed out or not that other easier ways might do the job as well, which may be doubtful, snow being snow, divinity divinity, holiness holiness, believing believing.

All alone at the rail he suddenly becomes conscious of the intense roaring of the silence, it fills his every ear and seems to permeate throughout the marble and the flowers and the darkening flickering air with the same pure hush transparency——The heaven heard sound for sure, hard as a diamond, empty as a diamond, bright as a diamond—— Like unceasing compassion its continual near-at-hand sea- wash and solace, some subtle solace intended to teach some subtler reward than the one we've printed and that for which the architects raised.

Enveloped in peaceful joy, my little brother hurries out the empty church and goes running and skampering home to supper thru raw marched streets.

"Did you go to your confession, Lil Gerard?"

"*Oui.*"

"Come eat, my golden angel, my *pitou,* my lil Mama's cabbage."

I'm sitting stupidly at a bed-end in a dark room realizing my Gerard is home, my mouth's been open in awe an hour you might think the way it's sorta slobbered and run down my cheeks, I look down to discover my hands upturned and loose on my knees, the utter disjointed inexistence of my bliss.

Me too I'd been hearing the silence, and seeing swarms of little lights thru objects and rooms and walls of rooms.

None of the elements of this dream can be separated from any other part, it is all one pure suchness.

Would I were divinest punner and tell how the cold winds blow with one stroke of my quick head in this harsh unhospitable hospital called the earth, where "thou owest God a death"——Time for me to get on my own horse——

The Kat is up on the sink actually fascinated by the drip drip of the faucet, there he is with his paws under him and his tail curling down and his ruminative quickglancing face bending and earpricking to the phenomena, as tho he was trying to figure out, or pass the time, or make fun of us——But Mama has a headache, it's a cold windy night in Old February and Pa is out late at work (playing poker backstage B.F.Keiths maybe with W.C.Fields for all I know with my drawn yawp masque)——The winds belabor at the windows of the kitchen, Ma is on the couch on the newspapers where she's flopped in despair, it's about 9:30, supper dishes have been put away (tenderly by her own hands) and now she lies there head back on a kewpie cushion with an ice pack on her head——The woodstove roars——Gerard and I are at the stove rocker, warming our feet, Nin is at the table doing her *"devoir"* (homework)——

"Mama you're sick," demurs Gerard with the gods, with his piteous voice, "what are we going to do."

"Aw it'll go away."

He goes over and lays his head against hers and waits to hear her cure——

"If I had some aspirins."

"I'll go get you some——at drugstore!"

"It's too late."

"It's only 9:30——I'm not afraid."

"Poor Lil Gerard it's too cold tonight and it's too late."

"No mama! I'll dress up good! My hat my rubbers!"

"Run. Go to Old Man Bruneau, ask him for a bottle of aspirin——the money is in my pocketbook."

Together Gerard and I peer and probe into the mysterious pocketbook for the mysterious nickles and dimes that are always there intermingled with rosaries and gum and powder puffs——

Little Gerard runs and puts his muffcap and draws it over his ears and draws on his rubbers with that tragic bent over motion no angels who never lived on earth could know ——A cold key in a tight lock, our situation, the skin so warm, thin, the night of Winter so broad and cool—— So Saskatchewan'd with advantage——

"Hurry up my golden, Mama'll be afraid——"

"I'll go get your medicine and you'll be all right, just watch!"

Gleefully he goes off, the door admits Spectre into the kitchen an instant and he slams it—I watch him tumble off.

Beaulieu Street going down towards West Sixth, 4 houses, to the Fire House, is swept by dusts——The lamp on the corner only serves to accentuate by contrast the lightlessness in the general air——The stars above are no help, they twinkle in a vain freeze——The cold sweeps down Gerard's neck, he tries to bundle in——He hurries around the corner and down West Sixth, towards the lights of the big corner at Aiken and Lilley and West Sixth where bleak graypaint tenements stand with dull brown kitchen lights under the hard stars——Not a soul in sight, a few cruds of old snow stuck in the gutters——A fine world for icebergs and stones ——A world not made for men——A world, if made for anything, made for something dead to sympathy——Since sympathizing there'll not be in it ever——He runs to warm up——

Down at Aiken the wind from the river hits him full-blast with a roar, around the corner, bringing with it the odor of cold rocks in the river's ice, and the savor of rust——

"God doesnt look like he made the world for people" he guesses all by himself as it occurs in his chilled bones the hopeless sensation——No help in sight, the utter help-less-ness up, down, around——The stars, rooftops, dusty swirls, streetlamps, cold storefronts, vistas at street-ends where you know the earthflat just continues on and on into a round February the roundness of which and warm ball of which wont be vouchsafed us Slav-level fools as but flat ——Flat as a tin pan——So for winds to swail across, a man oughta lie down on his back on a cold night and miss those winds——No thought, no hope of the mind can dispel, nay no millions in the bank, can break, the truth of the Winter night and that we are not made for this world——Stones yes, grass and trees for all their green return I'd say no to judge from their dead brownness tonight——A million may buy a hearth, but a hearth wont buy rich safety——

Gerard divines that all of this is pure division, a grief of separation, the cold is cold because there are two to know it, the cold and he who is en-colded——"If it wasnt for that, like in Heaven, . . ."

"And Mama has a headache, aw God why'd you do all this this suffering?"

En route back with the aspirins he hears a forlorn rumble in Ennell Street, it's the old junkman coming back from some over extended work somewhere in windswept junk-slopes, his horse is steaming, his steel-on-wood-wheels are grinding grit on grit and stone on stone and wind swirls dust about his burlaps, as he smiles that tooth-smile of the cold between embittered lips, you see the suffering of his mitts and the weeping in his beard, the woe——Going home to some leaky rafter——To count his rusty corsets and by-your-leaves and tornpaper accounts and pile-alls——To die on his heap of mistakes, finally, and what was gained in emptiness you'll never find debited or credited in any ac-count——What the preachers say not excepted——"Poor old man, he hasnt got a nice warm kitchen, he hasnt got a mother, he hasnt got a little sister and little brother and Papa, he's alone under the hole under the open stars—— If it was all together in one ball of wool——!——" The horse's hooves strike sparks, the wheels labor to turn into West Sixth, the whole shebang sorrows out of sight—— Gerard approaches our house, our golden kitchen lights and pauses on the cold porch for one last look up——The stars have nothing to do with anything.

In some other way, he hopes.

"There, your little hands are cold——thank you my child

——bring me a glass of water——I'll be all right——Mama's sick tonight——"

"Mama——why is it so cold?"

"Dont ask me."

"Why did God leave us sick and cold? Why didnt he leave us in Heaven."

"You 're sure we were there?"

"Yes, I'm sure."

"How are you sure?"

"Because it cant be like it is."

"*Oui*"——Ma in her rare moments when thinking seriously she doesnt admit anything that doesnt ring all the way her bell of mind——"but it is."

"I dont like it. I wanta go to Heaven. I wish we were all in Heaven."

"Me too I wish."

"Why cant we have what we want?" but as soon as he says that the tears appear in his eyes, as he knows the selfish demand——

"Aw Mama, I dont understand."

"Come come we'll make some nice hot chocolate!——"

"Hot chocolate! (*Du coco!*)" cries Ti Nin, and I echo it: "Klo Klo!"

The big cocoa deal boils and bubbles chocolating on the stove and soon Gerard forgets——

If his mortality be the witness of Gerard's sin, as Augustine Page One immediately announced, then his sin must have been a great deal greater than the sin of mortals who enjoy, millionaires in yachts a-sailing in the South Seas with blondes and secretaries and flasks and engineers and endless hormone pills and Tom Collins Moons and peaceful deaths ——The sins of the junkman on Ennell Street, they were vast almost as mine and brother's——

In bed that night he lies awake, Gerard, listening to the moan of wind, the flap of shutters——From where he lies he can just see one cold sparkle star——The fences have no hope.

Like, the protection you'd get tonight huddling against an underpass.

But Gerard had his holidays, they bruited before his wan smile ——New Year's Eve we're all in bed upstairs under the wall-papered eaves listening to the racket horns and rattlers below and out the window the dingdong bells and sad horizon hush of all Lowell and towards Kearney Square where we see the red glow embrowned and aura'd in the new (1925) sky and we think: "A new year"——A new year with a new number and a new little boy with candlelight and *kitchimise* standing radiant in the eternities, as the old, some old termagant with beard and scythe, goes wandering down the darkness field, and on the sofa arms of the parlor chairs even now the fairies are dancing——Gerard and Nin and I are sitting up in the one bed of conclave, with a happy smile he's trying to explain to us what's really happening but by and by the drunks come upstairs with wild hats to kiss us——Some sorrow involved in the crinkly ends of pages of old newspapers bound in old readingroom files so that you turn and see the news of that bygone New Year's day, the advertisements with top hats, the crowds in Hail streets, the snow——The little boy under the quilt who will have X's in his eyes when the rubber lamppost ushers in his latter New Years Eves, one scythe after another lopping off his freshness juices till he comes to bebibbling them from corny necks of bottles——And the swarm in the darkness, of an ethereal kind, where nobody ever looks, as if if they did look the swarms ethereal would wink off, winking, to wink on again when no one's watching——Gerard's bright explanations about dark time, and cowbells——Then we had our Easter.

Which came with lilies in April, and you had white doves in the fields, and we went seesawing thru Palm Sunday and we'd stare at those pictures of Jesus meek on the little *azno* entering the city and the palm multitudes, "The Lord has found that nice little animal there and he got up on his back and they rode into the city"——"Look, the people are all glad"——A few chocolate rabbits one way or the other was not the impress of our palmy lily-like Easter, our garland of roses, our muddy-earth Spring sigh when all in new shoes we squeaked to the church and outside you could smell the fragrant cigarettes and see men spit and inside the church was all dormant and adamant like wine with white white flowers everywhere——

We had our Fourth of July, some firecrackers, some fence sitting spitting of sparks, warm trees of night, boys throwing torpedoes against fences, general wars, oola-oo-ah popworks at the Common with the big bomb was the finale, and popcorn and Ah Lemonade——

And Halloween: the Halloween of 1925, when Ma dressed me up as a little Chinaman with a queu and a white robe and Gerard as a Pirate and Nin as a Vamp and old Papa took us by the hand and paraded us down to the corner at Lilley and Aiken, ice cream sodas, swarms of eyes on the sidewalks——

All the little children of the world keep quickly coming and going to the holidays that only slowly change, but the quality of the brightness of their eyes monotonously reverts ——Seeds, seeds, the seed sown everywhere blossoming the fruit of our loom, living-but-to-die——There's just no fun in holidays when you know.

All the living and dying creatures of the endless future wont even wanta be forewarned——wherefore, I should shut up and close up shop and bang shutters and broom my own dark and nasty nest.

At this time my father had gotten sick and moved part of his printing business in the basement of the house where he had his press, and upstairs in an unused bedroom where he had some racks of type——He had rheumatism too, and lay in white sheets groaned and saying *"La marde!"* and looking at his type racks in the next room where his helper Manuel was doing his best in an inkstained apron.

It was later on, about the time Gerard got really sick (long-sick, year-sick, his last illness) that this paraphernalia was moved back to the rented shop on Merrimack Street in an alley in back of the Royal Theater, an alley which I visited just last year to find unchanged and the old gray-wood Colonial one storey building where Pa's pure hope-shop rutted, a boarded up ghost-hovel not even fit for bums ——And forlorner winds never did blow ragspaper around useless rubbish piles, than those that blow there tonight in that forgotten alley of the world which is no more forgotten than the heartbreaking and piteous way Gerard had of holding his head to the side whenever he was interested or bemused in something, and as if to say, "Ay-you, world, what are our images but dust?——and our shops,"——sad.

Nonetheless, lots of porkchops and beans came to me via my old man's efforts in the world of business which for all the fact that 't is only the world of adult playball, procures tightwad bread from hidden cellars the locks of which are guarded by usurping charlatans who know how easy it is to enslave people with a crust of bread withheld—— He, Emil, went bustling and bursting in his neckties to find the money to pay rents, coalbills (for to vaunt off that selfsame winter night and I'd be ingrat to make light of it whenever trucks come early morning and dump their black and dusty coal roar down a chute of steel into our under bins)——Ashes in the bottom of the furnace, that Ma herself shoveled out and into pails, and struggled to the ashcan with, were ashes representative of Poppa's efforts and tho their heating faculties were in Nirvana now 'twould be loss of fealty to deny——I curse and rant nowaday because I dont want to have to work to make a living and do childish work for other men (any lout can move a board from hither to yonder) but'd rather sleep all day and stay it up all night scrubbling these visions of the world which is only an ethereal flower of a world, the coal, the chute, the fire and the ashes all, imaginary blossoms, nonetheless, "somebody's got to do the work-a the world"——Artist or no artist, I cant pass up a piece of fried chicken when I see it, compassion or no compassion for the fowl——Arguments that raged later between my father and myself about my refusal to go to work——"I wanta *write*——I'm an *artist*" ——"Artist shmartist, ya cant be supported all ya life——"

And I wonder what Gerard would have done had he lived, sickly, artistic——But by my good Jesus, with that holy face they'd have stumbled over one another to come and give him bread and breath——He left me his heart but not his tender countenance and sorrowful patience and kindly lights——

"Me when I'm big, I'm gonna be a painter of beautiful pictures and I'm gonna build beautiful bridges"——He never lived to come and face the humble problem, but he would have done it with that *noblesse tendresse* I never in my bones and dead man heart could ever show.

It's a bright cold morning in December 1925, just before Christmas, Gerard is setting out to school——Aunt Marie has him by the hand, she's visiting us for a week and she wants to take a morning constitutional, and take deep breaths and show Gerard how to do likewise, for his health——Aunt Marie is my father's favorite sister (and my favorite aunt), a talkative openhearted, teary bleary lovely with red lipstick always and gushy kisses and a black ribbon pendant from her specs——While my father has been abed with rheumatism she's helped somewhat with the housework——Crippled, on crutches, a modiste——Never married but many boyfriends helped her——The spittin image of Emil and the lover of Gerard's little soul as no one else, unless it be the cold eyed but warm hearted Aunt Anna from up in Maine——"Ti Gerard, for your health always do this, take big clacks of air in your lungs, hold it a long time, look" pounding her furpieced breast, "see?"——

"*Oui,* Matante Marie——"

"Do you love your Matante?"

"My Matante Marie I love her so big!" he cries affectionately as they hug and limp around the corner, to the school, where the kids are, in the yard, and the nuns, who now stare curiously at Gerard's distinguished aunt——Aunt Marie take her leave and drops in the church for a quick prayer ——It's the Christmas season and everyone feels devout.

The kids bumble into their seats in the classroom.

"This morning," says the nun up front, "we're going to study the next chapter of the catechism——" and the kids turn the pages and stare at the illustrations done by old French engravers like Boucher and others always done with the same lamby gray strangeness, the curlicue of it, the reeds of Moses' bed-basket I remember the careful way they were drawn and divided and the astonished faces of women by the riverbank——It's Gerard's turn to read after Picou'll be done——He dozes in his seat from a bad night's rest during which his breathing was difficult, he doesnt know it but a new and serious attack on his heart is forming ——Suddenly Gerard is asleep, head on arms, but because of the angle of the boy's back in front of him the nun doesnt see.

Gerard dreams that he is sitting in a yard, on some house steps with me, his little brother, in the dream he's thinking sorrowfully: "Since the beginning of time I've been charged to take care of this little brother, my Ti Jean, my poor Ti Jean who cries he's afraid——" and he is about to stroke me on the head, as I sit there drawing a stick around in the sand, when suddenly he gets up and goes to another part of the yard, nearby, trees and bushes and something strange and gray and suddenly the ground ends and there's just air and supported there at the earth's gray edge of immateriality, is a great White Virgin Mary with a flowing robe ballooning partly in the wind and partly tucked in at the edges and held aloft by swarms, countless swarms of grave bluebirds with white downy bellies and necks——On her breast, a crucifix of gold, in her hand a rosary of gold, on her head a star of gold——Beauteous beyond bounds and belief, like snow, she speaks to Gerard:

"Well my goodness Ti Gerard, we've been looking for you all morning——where were you?"

He turns to explain that he was with. . .that he was on . . . .that he was. . . .that. . .——He cant remember what it is that it was, he cant remember why he forgot where he was, or why the time, the morning-time, was shortened, or lengthened——The Virgin Mary reads it in his perplexed eyes. "Look," pointing to the red sun, "it's still early, I wont be mad at you, you were only gone less than a morning—— Come on——"

"Where?"

"Well, dont you remember? We were going——come on——"

"How'm I gonna follow you?"

"Well your wagon is there" and Oh yes, he snaps his finger and looks to remember and there it is, the snow-white cart drawn by two lambs, and as he sits in it two white pigeons settle on each of his shoulders; as prearranged, he bliss-remembers all of it now, and they start, tho one per-plexing frown shows in his thoughts where he's still trying to remember what he was and what he was doing before,

or during, his absence, so brief——And as the little wagon of snow ascends to Heaven, Heaven itself becomes vague and in his arm with head bent Gerard is contemplating the perfect ecstasy when his arm is rudely jolted by Sister Marie and he wakes to find himself in a classroom with the sad window-opening pole leaning in the corner and the erasers on the ledges of the blackboards and the surly marks of woe smudged thereon and the Sister's eyes astonished down on his:

"Well what are you doing Gerard! you're sleeping!"

"Well I was in Heaven."

"What?"

"Yes Sister Marie, I've arrived in Heaven!"

He jumps up and looks at her straight to tell her the news.

"It's your turn to read the catechism!"

"Where?"

"There——the chapter——at the end——"

Automatically he reads the words to please her; while pausing, he looks around at the children; Lo! all the beings involved! And look at the strange sad desks, the wood of them, and the carved marks on them, initials, and the little boy Ouellette (suddenly re-remembered) as usual with the same tranquil unconcern (outwardly) whistling soundlessly into his eraser, and the sun streaming in the high windows showing motes of room-dust——The whole pitiful world is still there! and nobody knows it! the different appearances of the same emptiness everywhere! the ethereal flower of the world!

"My sister, I saw the Virgin Mary."

The nun is stunned: "Where?"

"There——in a dream, when I slept."

She does the sign of the cross.

"Aw Gerard, you gave me a start!"

"She told me come on——and there was a pretty little white wagon with two little lambs to pull it and we started out and we were going to Heaven."

"Mon Seigneur!"

"A little white wagon!" echo several children with excitement.

"Yes——and two white pigeons on my shoulder—— doves——and she asked me 'Where were you Gerard, we've been waiting for you all morning' "——

Sister Marie's mouth is open——"Did you see all this in a dream?——? here now?——in the room."

"Yes my good sister——dont be afraid my good sister, we're all in Heaven——but we dont know it!"——"Oh," he laughs, *"we dont know it!"*

"For the love of God!"

"God fixed all this a long time ago."

The bell is ringing announcing the end of the hour, some of the children are already poised to scamper on a word,

Sister Marie is so stunned everyone is motionless——Gerard sits again and suddenly over him falls the tight overpowering drowsiness around his heart, as before, and his legs ache and a fever breaks on his brow——He remains in his seat in a trance, hand to brow, looking up minutes later to an empty room save for Soeur Marie and the elder Soeur Caroline who has been summoned——They are staring at him with tenderest respect.

"Will you repeat what you told me to Sister Caroline?"

"Yes——but I dont feel good."

"What's the matter, Gerard?"

"I'm starting to be sick again I guess."

"We'll have to send him home——"

"They'll put him to bed like they did last year, like before——He hasnt got much strength, the little one."

"He saw Heaven."

"Ah"——shrugging, Sister Caroline——"that"——nodding her head——

Slowly, at 9:30 o'clock that morning, my mother who's in the yard with clothespins in her mouth sees him coming down the empty schooltime street, alone, with that lassitude and dragfoot that makes a chill in her heart——

"Gerard is sick——"

For the last time coming home from school.

When Christmas Eve comes a few days later he's in bed, in the side room downstairs——His legs swell up, his breathing is difficult and painful——The house is chilled. Aunt Louise sits at the kitchen table shaking her head——*"La peine, la peine,* pain, pain, always pain for the Duluozes ——I knew it when he was born——his father, his aunt, all his uncles, all invalids——all in pain——Suffering and pain ——I tell you, Emil, we havent been blessed by Chance."

The old man sighs and plops the table with his open hand. "That goes without saying."

Tears bubbling from her eyes, Aunt Louise, shifting one hand quickly to catch a falling crutch, "Look, it's Christmas already, he's got his tree, his toys are all bought and he's lying there on his back like a corpse——it's not *fair* to hurt little children like that that arent old enough to know—— Ah Emil, Emil, Emil, what's going to happen, what's going to happen to *all* of us!"

And her crying and sobbing gets me crying and sobbing and soon Uncle Mike comes in, with wife and the boys, partly for the holidays, partly to see little Gerard and offer him some toys, and he too, Mike, cries, a great huge tormented tearful man with bald head and blue eyes, asthmatic thunderous efforts in his throat as he draws each breath to expostulate long woes: "My poor Emil, my poor little brother Emil, you have so much trouble!" followed by crashing coughs and in the kitchen the other aunt is saying to my mother:

"I told you to take care of him, that child——he was never strong, you know——you've always got to send him warmly dressed" and et cetera as tho my mother had somehow been to blame so she cries too and in the sickroom Gerard, waking up and hearing them, realizes with compassion heavy in his

heart that it is only an ethereal sorrow and too will fade
when heaven reveals her white.

"*Mon Seigneur,*" he thinks, "bless them all"——

He pictures them all entering the belly of the lamb——
Even as he stares at the wood of the windowframe and the
plaster of the ceiling with its little cobwebs moving to the
heat.

Hearken, amigos, to the olden message: it's neither what
you think it is, nor what you think it isnt, but an elder
matter, uncompounded and clear——Pigs may rut in
field, come running to the Soo-Call, full of sow-y glee;
people may count themselves higher than pigs, and walk
proudly down country roads; geniuses may look out of windows and count themselves higher than louts; tics in the
pine needles may be inferior to the swan; but whether any
of these and the stone know it, it's still the same truth: none
of it is even there, it's a mind movie, *believe* this if you will
and you'll be saved in the solvent solution of salvation and
Gerard knew it well in his dying bed in his way, in his way
——And who handed us down the knowledge here of the
Diamond Light? Messengers unnumberable from the
Ethereal Awakened Diamond Light. And why?——because
is, is——and was, was——and will be, will be—t'will!

Christmas Eve of 1925 Ti Nin and I gayly rushed out
with our sleds to a new snow layer in Beaulieu street, for-

getting our brother in his sack, tho it was he sent us out with injunctions to play good and slide far——

"Look at the pretty snow outside, go play!" he cried like a kindly mother, and we bundled up and went out——

I still remember the quality of that sky, that very evening, tho I was only 3 years old——

Over the roofs, which held their white and would hold them all night now that the sun was casting himself cold and wan-pink over the final birches of griefstricken westward Dracut——Over the roofs was that blue, magic Lowell blue, that keen winter northern knifeblade blue of winter dusks so unforgettable and so cold and dry, like dry ice, flint, sparks, like powdery snow that ss'ses at under doorsills ——Perfect for the silhouetting of birds heading darkward down their appointed lane, hushed——Perfect for the silhouetting presentations of church steeples and of rooftops and of the whole Lowell general, and always yon poor smoke putting from the human chimneys like prayer—— The whole town aglow with the final russet adventures of the day staining windowpanes and sending pirates to the east and bringing other sabers of purple and of saffron scarlet harlot rage across the gashes and might ironworks of incomprehensible moveless cloud wars frowned and befronting one another on horizon Shrewsburies——Up there where instead of thickening, plots thinned and leaked and warrior groups pulled wan expiring acts on the monstrous rugs of sky areas with names in purple, and dull boom cannons, and maw-mouth awwp up-clouds far far away where the children say "There's an old man sleeping in the north with a big white mouth that's open and a round nose"—— These mighty skies bending over Lowell and over Gerard as he lay knowing in his deathbed, rosaries in his hands, pans on papers by the bed, pillows under his feet——The sides and portion wedges of which sky he can barely see thru the window shade and frame, outside is December's big parley with night and it's Christmas Eve and his heart breaks to realize that it will be his last Christmas on our innocent mistaken earth——"Ah yes——if I could tell them what I knew——but when I start it stops coming, it's gone, it's not to talk about——but now I *know* it——just like my dream——poor people with their houses and their chimnies and their Christmases and their children——listen to them yelling in the street, listen to their sleds——they run, they throw themselves on the snow, the little sled takes them a little ways and then that's all——that's all——And me, big nut, I cant explain them what they're dying to know——It's because God doesnt wanta——"

God made us for His glory, not our own.

Nin and I have our sleds and mufflers and we have wrangled dramas with the other kids over the little dispositions of activity among snowbanks and slide-lanes, it all goes on endlessly this world in its big and little facets with no change in it.

In the kitchen, before Pa gets home and in a quiet in-
terim when Gerard's asleep and we're still sliding, Ma
takes out her missal and unfolds a paper from it on which
are written the words of the prayer to St. Martha:——

"St. Martha, I resort to thy protection and aid and as proof
of my affection and faith I offer this light which I shall burn
every Tuesday."

She lights her devotional candle.

"Comfort me in difficulties and thru the great favor which
you enjoyed thru lodging in the house of Our Saviour, inter-
cede for my family that we may always hold God in our
hearts and be provided for in our necessities. I beseech thee
to have infinite pity in regard to the favor I ask thee."
(State favor).

"If you please, my Lord, bless my poor little Gerard and
make him well again, so he can live his little life in peace
——and without pain——he has suffered so much——he's
suffered enough for twenty four old sick men and he hasnt
said a word——My Lord, have pity on this little courageous
child, amen."

"I ask thee, St. Martha," she finishes reading the prayer,
"to overcome all difficulties as thou didst overcome the
dragon which thou hadst at your feet. Our Father——Hail
Mary——Glory Be"——

And at that very moment ladies in black garments, scores
of them, are scattered throughout St. Louis de France church,
kneeling or sitting or some standing at the various special
shrines, their lips muttering prayers for similar requests for

similar troubles in their own poor lives and if indeed the
Lord seeth all and saw all that is going on and all the
beseechment in His name in dark earth-churches throughout the kingdom of consciousness, it would be with pain
He'd attend and bend His thoughts to it——Some of the
women are 80 years old, they've been coming to that basement church at dusk every day for the last quarter of a
century and they've had manifold and O manifold reasons
to loft prayer from that cellar, little chance they mightnt——

Amazing how the kids always scream with glee around
the church at that sad hour of dusk.

And by God, amazing the bar standers and beer eaters
bubbling at elbow bangs in speakeasy clubs around the corner, enough to make a man believe in Rabelais and Khayyam
and throw the Bible and the Sutras and the dry Precepts
away——"*Encore un autre verre de bière mon Christ de
vieux matou!* Another glass a beer ya Christing old he-cat!"

"Well you're swearing like a dog on Christmas Eve!"

"Christmas Eve my——my you-know-what, if I dont have
a glass a beer in my belly and two hundred others to boot
it dont render *me* no merry in the Merry Christmas even
if there was forty of your Christmases in the calendar the
same bloody day I'm talkin to ya," translation to that effect.
"*Calvert, Caribou est sou,* Caribou's drunk!"

"Drunk? Come to my house, I got some whiskey there

that'll make you fill your words with another kinda *marde!*"

The cussingest people in the world the Canucks in their cups, all you have to do is go to their capital and range up and down the bars of Ste. Catherine Street in Montreal to see some guzzling and some profanity.

"Gayo, sonumbitch, go shit!"

"Ah the bastat."

A pretty Christmas they're having, there's a little tree in the corner with lights, and drunk under it——In comes the younger element, they'll have to take out papers to catch up with the old good swigglers and cussmakers——

My father, en route home, stops for a quick one himself in the company of his old friend Gaston MacDonald who has a spanking 1922 Stutz parked outside, with them is Manuel whose usual courtesy of driving Pa home tonight in the sidecar motorcycle has been set aside in favor of the Stutz and besides it's too cold and besides they're so high now the motorcycle trip would have been a fatality——

"Drink, Emil, amuse yourself, dammit it's Christmas!"

"Not for me, Gaston——with my little Gerard in bed it's not a hell of a pretty Christmas."

"Ah, he was sick before."

"Yes but it always tears my heart out."

"Ah well, poor Emil, you might as well go throw yourself on the rocks in the river off the cliff in Little Canada. . .to crack. . .your spirit like that——look here, nothin you can do. Down the hatch!"

"Down the hatch."

"You dammit Manuel I thought you was s'posed to be a drunkard?"

"Drunkards take their time," says my father's assistant with a sly grin——

There are also silent drinkers with big chapped red fists around silent glasses, huddled over, figuring out ways to get their wives outa their thoughts and you can see their mouths lengthen down and draw sorrow almost as you look——

"Poor dog there, look, Bolduc,——do you know that guy was the best basketball player at the YMCA in '18?——and '16, and '17 too!——They offered him a professional contract ——No, his father didnt want it, old rocky Rocher Bolduc, 'Stay in your store damn you or you'll never have it again' ——today he's got the store, little candies for the children, licorice, pencils, a little stove near the corner, Bolduc spends his time in there with his sweater and his wife hates him and there was a time when he was the biggest athlete in Lowell——and a goodlooking happygolucky guy!"

And chances are Bolduc's wife is one of the black sorrowful ladies in the now-dark pews a few blocks up from the club——

My father has his drink, two or three of them, and wipes his mouth, and heads home, on foot passing thru the corner at Lilley and Aiken, stopping at the drugstore for his 7-20-4 cigars, then the bakery for fresh Franco-American bread that at home he'll slice on a wood board in the middle of the table slices big enough to write your biography on——

"Allo Emil——long time no see."

"I'm pretty busy."

"Still got your shop near the Royal?"

"I'm established there, Roger—business is going good."

"The *anglais* aint givin you *marde?*" (the English)——
"the Irish——the Greeks?——one thing me I like about
bread, I do my business with the Canadians" (pronounced
Ca-na-yen, the thick peasant pride and emphatic umph of
it)——

My father is actually a complicated cosmopolite compared
to Roger the baker——but he hands him a cigar.

"We'll see you at the bazaar?"

"If I have time——I'll pitch in a little in any case, for
invitation cards, my little bit——"

And all the usual pleasantries, detailed styles, and pano-
ramic shots of a complete social scene, Centerville in Lowell
in 1925 being a close knit truly French community such
as you might not find any more (with the peculiar Medieval
Gaulic closed-in flavor) in modern long-eared France——

Emil comes home with his cigars and bread, and rounds
the corner of Beaulieu just as the dusk clouds have fought
their last war grim and purple in the invisibilities and here
comes the evening star shimmering like a magic hanger in
the fade-far flank of the retreat, and lights of brown and
quiet flavor have come on in homes and he sees lil Nin and
I wheeing with our sleds——

"In any case I got two of em in good health——but in
my heart I cant be happy about anything, Gerard there are

no others like Gerard, I shall never be able to understand where a little boy like that got so much goodness——so much——enough to make me cry, damn it——it's the way he's always got his little head to one side——pensive, so sad, so concerned——I'd give all the Lowells for the map of the Devil, to keep my Gerard——Will I keep him?" he wonders looking up?——seeing the same unsaying stars Gerard had stared at——"*Mystère,* it's a Christmas to make the dogs cry"——"Come my little kids!" he calls to Nin and me but we dont hear him in the heat of our play in the cold snow so he goes in the house anyway, with that sad motion of men passing into their domiciles, the pitifulness of it, specially in winter, the sight of which, if an angel returned from heaven and looked (if angels, if heaven, which is an ethereal crock) would make an angel melt——If angels were angels in the first place.

Christmas comes, Gerard gets a great new erector set, big enough and complicated enough to build hoists that'll carry the house away——He sits in bed contemplating it with his little sad sideways look, like the way the moon looks on May nights, the face tilted over——It's an expression, with his arms folded, that again and again says "Ah, but and but, look at that, my souls"——Nin gets a pickaninny doll, I remember distinctly finding it that Christmas morning on the mantle by the tree, and the little high chair that went with it, and Gerard promptly that week made a little doll house for his sister, subsidiary gifts from his own Santa Claus hands——Me, I had toys that I've forgotten cold, and it goes to show——

Then New Year's——

Then the bleak January, the friendless February with his iron fingers in your grill of ribs——

Gerard lay abed all the time, getting up only to go to the toilet or occasional wan visits to the breakfast table, where after dishes were cleared, he'd sometimes sit a half hour erecting structures high that I watched standing at the side of him, holding his knee I expect——"What you doin, Gerard?"

No answer but in the action of his hands and the working of his face as he thinks, and I marvel at my love for him——

Then he'd get tired and sigh and go back to bed and try to sleep, at midday, and I had no one to play with any more——I'd bring him drawingboards and crayons, he'd feebly rise to do my bidding——Sitting up, against pillows, legs out, in the white room, and white frost on the windowpane, and my mother watching us in the doorway—— Her gleeful way of saying: "You're having fun now?" as tho everything was alright with the world and 50 years later she'll still be the same, and seen it all——

"Ti Pousse, Ti Pousse, Ti Pousse, how fat you are Ti Pousse," he'd say to me, mockfighting and hugging me and stroking my face. "Little Cabbage, Little Wolf, Little Piece of Butter, Little Boy, Little Pile, Little Nut, Little Savage,

Little Bad, Little Cryer, Little Bawler, Little Winner, Little Robber, Little Lazy, Little *Kitigi*——Ti Jean Ti Jean—— *Ti Jean Louis le gros Pipi*——Little Fatty——you weigh two tons—they'll bring you in a truck——Little Red, Little red mug——Look, Mama, the beautiful red cheeks Ti Jean has ——he'll be handsome little boy!——he'll be strong!"

I basked in all this just like you would expect someone who deserved it, to bask in eternal bliss——I was going to be made to appreciate it, like a Fallen Angel.

Lancing pain in the legs and vague pain in the chest wakes Gerard in the mid of night, he makes a soft groan and represses even that realizing we're all asleep, and Mama is exhausted——I lie in the crib across the room, lips to sheet——"Aw it hurts, it hurts!!" he groans, and grabs his pain, which wont stop——It comes on and off like a light.

"Lance, lance, lance, why is this happening to me, what'd I do? I confessed to the priest, I havent hidden anything—— It's not that——Aw well, I guess it isnt worth it living—— Ow——Oh Ow——" Hands to face, about to cry. Like a load of rocks dumped from a truck onto a little kitty, the pitiful inescapability of death and the pain of death, and it will happen to the best and all and most beloved of us, O—— Why should such hearts be made to wince and cringe and groan out life's breath?———*why does God kill us?*———The only answer can be written without words.

And Gerard knows that. He remembers his whole life now. Nothing to do in the long pain night, but hurt. And think. It is the long night of life. And think. The morning he was born somehow there was gray rain and damp overshoes and rubbers in a dreary closet and a brown sad light in the kitchen and angry smirch of bepestered life-faces, and somehow from somewhere out, or in the center, Counsel coming to him, saying, "Dont do it———Dont be born" but he was born, he wanted to do it and be born and ignored the Counsel, the Ancient Counsel———

The pain knifes into his jerking flesh, he jumps in bed a little, and aside, to avoid, it fades away a bit———"To me, to me it's happening"———He knows it isnt happening to me otherwise I'd be thrashing in my crib———"It's happening only to me"———He hears Pa snore upstairs, the littler harmonious snores of probably Ti Nin and Ma———It's only happening to him and it's the middle of the night and the window leaks and rattles from that wind———Out on the cold canals of Lowell across the river, snow-swirls are turning in the moon———

"O, when will it stop———?"

"O my Lord, help me———"

A stab of pain———"Help me!" he involuntarily cries out loud———"Nobody could know how much it hurts———O my Jesus you've left me alone and you're hurting me———And you too, you were hurted———Aw Jesus———nothing to help me——nothing"——Stab of strange pain, it advertises as it comes and comes with quick and open robbery, and vanishes with your peace——"I'll have to die, I'll have to die!" steals the dark cant-help-it thought——"If it doesnt stop"——And *It wont stop* sneaks the other thought, coming with the pain as voucher——

"Throughout all that, throughout that snowy window and the cold night and the big wind, and my leg and everything else in the house, throughout all that there isnt something else?"

And ecstasy unfolds inside his mind like a flower and says Yes, and he sees millions of white dots, like, and in another instant his legs are stabbing again and he's opened his eyes to concentrate on the concentrating——Like a Roman Soldier left to die on a deserted battlefield and howling for mercy for three days running, without food or water, and finally dying, which is a remembrance of the great American Saint Edgar Cayce (according to him in an earlier transmigration) Gerard a petallish thing of 9 is left to face cold unhopeful bone antagonized deep by elements within itself that will to war and wreck it, he himself, his personal-soul, is but victimized, tyrannized, wracked, flung aside, suffered to be a loser in the dubious game of mortal well-being——Words cant do it——"I've been thrown to that!" ——A thousand realizations come to him——"It's got to stop!" the constant human thought as pain continues to hurt——

Words cant do it, readers will get sick of it——
Because it's not happening to themselves——

"O Lord, Ethereal Flower,
Messenger from Perfectness,
Hearer and Answerer of Prayer,
Raise thy diamond hand,
Bring to naught,
Destroy,
Exterminate—

O thou Sustainer,
Sustain all who are in extremity—

Bless all living and dying things in
    the endless past of the ethereal flower,
Bless all living and dying things in
    the endless present of the ethereal flower,
Bless all living and dying things in
    the endless future of the ethereal flower,
                                        amen."

Unceasing compassion flows from Gerard to the world even while he groans in the very middle of his extremity.

But comes morning and a temporary cessation of his pain and Ma's up making oatmeal in the kitchen, the steam from the stove is fragrant and comes and steams Gerard's bedroom window and gives everything a wonderful new quality of gladness, of simple attempt——The earth and the flesh be harsh, but there's comradeship below——"I'm making you some nice oatmeal, Gerard, and some nice toasts——wait another five minutes, I'll put you that on a tray and we'll have a nice breakfast together."

"It was a long night, Mama."

"Well now it's finished, my golden angel——It was hurting?"

"*Oui*"——sadly.

"You shoulda called me if it was hurting——Always call me when you need something, Mama is there——There! Ti Pousse is awake——your chum's gonna get up and you can spend the morning having fun together."

"O Mama, I'm so happy it's morning——the oatmeal smells so good——You're so nice, Mama."

Such tributes few mothers hear, or at least over so little, and over the oatmeal she blurs and rubs her eyes——"Dear angel, are you comfortable?——here, I'll fix your pillow——there"——slapping the pillow expertly, then kissing him——"There——Mama's golden angel——Dont worry, you'll be all better in two months——the Doctor Simpkins told me ——You'll be able to go out and play in the nice warm weather!——It'll be March in two weeks and *bing,* April! ——May!——See how fast it goes?"

"*Oui,* Ma."

"Dont you worry, with your Mama to take care of you you'll be well in two shakes of a lamb's tail——"

Great joy, because of the vacuum created by great horror

in the night, floods into his being as he sees his delighted mother come hurrying over bearing the steaming tray to place on his lap——Ahead of him is a long day of interested drawing and erector set——The sun hasnt shown, it's a cold cloudy day, the windows are gray and portentous with the news of the excitement of life and the healthy and the living——

He eats daintily and formally the simple food, reverencing each bite as tho it was holy, to enjoy it more, and because it is so momentous. "The corner of the toast——good—— the middle of the toast——there——" A faint twinge in his legs recalls the pain of the night before, and setting the tray aside with a weary sigh he nevertheless sees it fit to realize, "Ah well, it goes up and down and then it goes no more. It's best not to frighten anyone, nor harm anyone——dont let them know."

I'm up in my crib, in long johns, jealous because Gerard got his breakfast before me. I'm thinking "Because he's sick he's always waited on before me——Me, me!" I cry. "Me too I'm hungry!" "They always make such a fuss over him," I pout——I remember that morning, distinctly, standing in the crib like that——*Sticks and stones may break my bones but words'll hurt me never?*

In fact, Gerard is a little impatient with me for rattling the crib and throws me an exasperated look——"*Eh twé,* Oh you!"

And there's no doubt in my heart that my mother loves Gerard more than she loves me.

After awhile Pa's up and grumbling in the kitchen over his breakfast, with puffed disinterested eyes, not, as Edgar Cayce explicitly reminds us, "mindful of the present vision before our eyes."

The long night of life is terribly long and deceptively short.

Caribou the man who was drunkest and gayest the night before, having undergone indescribably ghastly feelings under the bridge where he wobbled and woggled and spit, is now lofting a new morning drink to his lips which will soon plunge him back into——what?

"What else you want me to do?——We all die? We're all piles of you-know-what? Liars? Poor? Invalids? Well then! I drink! Open the door, belly, gimme another chance." He gets his other chance, dances jigs till ten, and sleeps at noon. What he does at 4 o'clock in the afternoon is in its poor selfsame essence no different than what the mournful ladies with their beads and moving-lips, in the shadows of the church, are doing——For, the truth that is realizable in dead men's bones ought to be a good enough truth for everybody, laughers, cryers, cynics, and hopers included, all ——The truth that is realizable in dead men's bones, all great gloomy unwilling life aside, and setting aside my knighthood to thus say so, exhilirates yea exterminates all symbols and bosses and crosses and leaves that quiet blank ——For my part, the news about the truth came from the silence of my predecessor diers' graves.

Sicken if you will, this gloomy book's foretold.

Comes the cankerous rush of spring, when earth will fecundate and get soft and produce forms that are but to die, multiply——And a thousand splendors sweep across the March sky, and moons with raving moons that you see through drunken pine boughs snapping——When the river with her loaden humus gets heavier at the bank, because of the melting of the caky stiffnesses that'd had the earth seal-locked in her vaunted tomb of Hard——And there'll be laughter in the melting earth tonight——And there'll be sawdust, trees, women's thighs, river bends, star-light, backporches, more babies, young husbands, beer—— There'll be singing in the April tree tops——There'll be visitations from the South from oft-returning species of visitors with feather tails and beady eyes, avaricious for the worm——And the worm himself will divide into a billion counterparts and come oozing out of parted-sands (black and oily and blue) like as if someone were squeezing the earth from below——There'll be new fish——There'll be There'll-be Himself——

All of a sudden tossed wars of tree-tops will be warmer wars and less dry and crackety ones, and there'll be rumors and singing down the hillsides as snow melts, running for cover under the bloody light, to join the river's big body—— So that Ocean will again receive her swollen rent, as ever April, yet, landlord without end, be none the richer and

with such coffers bottomless how the poorer possible?——
In the ocean there is a Spring, deep and verdurous we cant
estimate, so I sing the surface one, the Spring that makes
us feel so sad and fair, and morning air brings nostalgic
cigarette smoke from holy hopey smokers——When hats
are whipped and finally succumb, coats flap and run their
stories out, and vests disappear, and shirtsleeves are hoisted
of a sudden afternoon April 26 and the ballgame is on——
The time when all the earth is black with sap——No end
to what you could say about Spring, and in that locked-in
New England Spring is a big event, long coming, short
staying, it flows by as fast as a flooded river——In that river
you can see the accumulated debris of seventeen thousand
fecundities up the both shores clear to the maw of the well
where she began——Marble'd melt in such country at the
time, and add veins to the color in the river——Children
run out exhilarated as princes and knights, illustriously
insane as ancient fools, to weirdly fool in fields and down
river banks; to at that time put them behind a knife-carved
schooldesk is like asking Thane to stow his Ice Axe and
say farewell to his Prow——It is the dizzy lyrical time, airy,
ethereal, mists are bright, the sun is never exactly golden,
never exactly silver, never exactly bright, never exactly dark,
never for a long time dimmed, but races continual eye dazzling wars, reaches everywhere throughout textures of clouds
and shows birds' shining wings——And when the first buds
appear on bushes and trees, and your heartborne blossoms
float to commemorate new Awakened Ones and fall in mig-

holes and on hopskotch trails, Vaya, then, night coming, and the round horizon all about reverberates with roars of all-sigh all-world all-men Shush War, you'll know, by the fence, the sad wooden American fences and under the promised yellow moon, the pierce of the arrow of April in your flesh, the promise accounted for in the Tablets of Hardworking Man's Beardy Serious Prophets: namely, ecstasy of living and dying...

You'll have your cold wars and warm peaces, the frotting and rubbings of all things on all sides, the ecstasy general, orgasms, screams of passion, rites of Spring, May, June, July and the Bees——No matter what anyone says, you'll have it, you'll dream you have it and so like the popular lovesong says, You'll Have It.

Blossoms fluttered from the trees and crossed contrarious Gerardo's windowpane, he would not balmy truck with Spring and swell with it, but wasted like Sacrosanct and ill-timed Autumn, out of his element——Like my father exactly 20 years later, he was dying during the Resurrection and the Life Renewed.

He was getting worse. Rarely now we saw him out of bed and about the kitchen. Our visits to his beside were still, for he slept a lot. My mother grew rings around her sleepless eyes, and prayed late and rose early to praise early——Her nerves were so shot she was losing her teeth one by one, her stomach was a mass of gelid anxious phenomena, like swarms of snakes——The Snake of Inevitability was rising up and eating the Duluozes.

My father had more time to avoid the sight of his little boy's death, by busying by burying himself in details of his work at the shop——And as heartbreaking April blossomed-burst into May and the mornings and the nights were music, the death in the house grew browner——I remember Spring-night the fence in our backyard, and the dim light in Gerard's sickroom window casting a faint candle-like glow on the lilac bushes, and above the warm teary stars, and the roar furor all around in the city of Lowell: trains across the river, the river itself booming heavily at the Falls, cries of people, doors slamming clear down to Lilley Street.

"Angie, we gotta do some work tonight me and Manuel ——I'm going to his house now."

"Awright Emil——dont come home too late——I'm afraid to be alone if anything happened."

"Ah well, you should be used to it by now——It'll happen in time."

"Dont talk like that——He recovered the last time."

"Yeah, but I never saw him skinny and quiet like that——Ah," from the porch, door open, "the beautiful nights that are coming——all for other people——"

"Call Ti Jean, he's in the yard with his kitty——it's his bedtime."

"Take it easy, my girl, I'll be home before eleven——We got a big order, just came in this morning——Manuel's waiting——Ti Jean, come in the house——your mother wants you——come on, my little man."

"Did you take your bath?"

"Aw tomorrow, if I'm dirty I'm dirty——Make me some *cortons* if you got time, I always like them for my sandwiches at the shop——"

"Bye Emil."

"Bye Angie——I'm going now."

Emil Alcide Duluoz, born in upriver St. Hubert Canada in 1889, I can picture the scene of his baptism at some wind whipped country crossing Catholic church with its ironspike churchspire high up and the paisans all dressed up, the bleak font (brown, or yellow, likely) where he is baptized, to go with the color of old teeth in this wolfish earth—Forlorn, the Plains of Abraham, the winds bring plague dust from all the way to Baffin and Hudson and where roads end and the Iroquois Arctic begins, the utterly hopeless place to which the French came when they came to the New World, the hardness of the Indians they must have embrothered to be able to settle so and have them for conspirators in the rebellion against contrarious potent churly England——Winds all the way from the nostril of the moose, coarse rough tough needs in potato fields, a little fold of honey enfleshed is being presented to the holy water for life——I can see all the kinds of Duluozes that must have been there that 1889 day, Sunday most likely, when Emil Alcide was anointed for his grave, for the earth's an intrinsic grave (just dig a hole and see)——Maybe Armenagé Duluoz, bowlegged 5 feet tall, plank-stiff, baptismal best boots, tie, chain and watch, hat (hat slopey, Saxish, slouch)——His statuesque and beauteous sisters in endless fold-draperies designed by Montreal couturiers tinkling delighted laughter late of afternoons when parochial children make long shadows in the gravel and Jesuit Brothers rush, bookish like "ill angels," from darkness to darkness——The mystery there for me, of Montreal the Capital and all French Canada the culture, out of which came the original potato paternity that rioted and wrought us the present family-kids of Emil——I can see the baptism of my father in St. Hubert, the horses and carriages, an angry tug at the reins, *"Allons ciboire de cawlis de calvert,* wait'll they finish wipin im"——Poor Papa Emil, and then began his life.

A whole story in itself, the story of Emil, his mad brothers and sisters, the whole troop coming down from the barren farm, to the factories of U.S.A.——Their early life in early Americana New Hampshire of pink suspenders, strawberry blondes, barbershop quartets, popcorn stands with melted butter in a teapot, and fistfights in the Sunday afternoon streets between bullies and heroes who read Frank Merri-well——Of Emil much later more——

But his rise from riotous family, to insurance salesman in the "big city" (for Lowell 14 miles downriver) and then to independent businessman with a shop, his waxing and puffing on cigars——His eager bursting out of vests and coats, tortured armpits of suits, quick short heavy steps on our history sidewalks——But a reverend, sensitive, apt-to-understand man, and understand he did, the mournfulness of his vision, the way he shook his head (that little Gerard imitated), the way he sighed——A citizen of the raving world, but eager to be good——Eager to be rich too——But a man endowed with qualities of interested apperception of the nature of things, as would qualify him to be a tragic philosopher——Insights, sadnesses, that leapfrogged his intelligence and came down on the other side and were light——"I see blind light——I see this sad black earth!" might have been one thought he had.

Here he goes hurrying to Manuel's for their night's work ——Manuel lives four blocks down near the big corner of Lilley and Aiken——As Emil turns off Beaulieu, which is the little street that bears the great burden of Gerard's dying, a breeze blows, bringing whiffs of hope, voices, song, it's a gay Saturday night, but the young father has no primer for that wellknown pump and only slowly ghostly sadly wends his way, thinking, "My father died drunk behind his stove——my mother died in her dishes and poor washclothes——father and mother, it happens to all of us one way or the other, we can pray if we want but it wont help ——Go on, God, dont call yourself God in my face——Doin business under conditions like that, we'll never win——"

Manuel lives in a raucous tenement, first floor, you walk in from the woodporch which has rollers that run the washlines across a tar court to the porch of the other tenements, all closed in, with, on warm Spring Night, all windows open and families airing their rave and grievance——Crash! Old Paquette's drunk again——Bang! Old lady Pirouette who lost her son in the war is dropping her dishes again—— Boom! that damn little Petrie's poppin off his lastyear's fire-crackers——It swims in thru all windows and revolves around and rumors and runs like a river, voices, language, gossip, crashes, jingles and jangles——"There's no end to it!"——Whole rant-sentences can be heard in rising and fall-ing snatches of vigorous Canuckois, coming from by old woodstoves in ancient rockingchairs——Sounds for the quick head and trailing robe——Emil walks in to Manuel's kitchen unannounced, nobody in it, he stands questioning——It doesnt take long for him to realize that Manuel is in the bedroom with his wife having a fight——

"They always told me not to marry you, you were a drunkard at sixteen——*sixteen?!!* I bet you was drunk as a hoot-owl at 15, 14——You're not the man I married but dammit the reason for that is because you were puttin up a front *when* I married you, crook——"

"Aw shut ya big ga dam mouth, it's only good for *blagues*——I gave you your money, I'm goin to work, I'll be gone all night, you oughta be satisfied, ya cow——"

"Dont call me a cow, dog——"

"Call yourself what you like, me I'm goin——and if I'm drunk tomorrow morning when I get back we'll blame it on you"——

"Aw yeah, look for excuses."

"Bein in the same house with a pest like you it's enough to make a man drink poison!"

"Why dont you do it then."

"And leave you my insurance that I took out because Emil Duluoz bullshitted my ear in 1920, not a chance——I'll live and you'll be poor——Go tell *that* to your mother."

My old man winces in the kitchen and bathetically would tiptoe out except that Manuel's wife is suddenly exploding into the kitchen with a backward added yell to loverboy: "Aw sure, simpleton, I'll go tell all this to my mother and make her happy she had a little girl and brought her up to well my goodness Mr. Duluoz is here!"

My father, eyes to the ceiling, salutes at the side of his head, as if to say "Dont mind me, I'm the court jester."

Manuel comes out of his gloomy bridalchamber with a chamberpot in his hand, and slippers on his feet. "Ah—— Emil——"

"Come on, Manuel, before Rosie throws you out on your face——"

"I'll throw him out to the Devil, damn him!" she screams, slamming the door that leads to the parlor which is never used.

(Sigh) my old man, "At least you dont have any children ——Put on your shoes and come on——You got drunk again there yesterday?"

"Just a little nip."

"Poor Manuel, come on I'll *buy* you a little nip—just one hour of work then we'll go to the club."

"How is it at home?"

"Well, there we dont fight, we——" he was about to say "we die" but checked himself.

Together they leave the tenement and get on Manuel's motorcycle with the side car, Emil in it, stately with hat-in-hand and goopy look, and off they go put-putting and bouncing over the Aiken Street Bridge——Almost exhilaration sweeps over both of them as the river winds whip their faces, and they both yell and point at the moon, which is rising yellow-huge on the horizon over Pawtucketville—— About a mile to the left are the glowing windows of the mills, some windows dye-blue, all reflected on the thrashy waters——About a mile to the right, Pawtucketville's hill of houses and the moon and one vast darkness cloud burlying over Spring——

It's the time of the juices——

They go careering up Aiken thru the tenement streets of Little Canada and cross the canal bridge and along to the high Medieval granite walls of St. Jean de Baptiste church (where Gerard was baptized), then left on Moody Street along busy storefronts, then right, to Merrimack Street, with its trolleys and busy cars, and down to the bright corner where stands the Jewel Theater, and the Royal Theater—— Manuel roars to a stop, they get out like brave mechanics, and toddle off down the alley by the Royal, redbrick, past the fire escape, to the rear——Emil turns on the light—— You see the press, the hand presses, the piles of glossy paper, the paper cutter, the roll-trucks, the inky shadows, rolls,

rags, cans, inks, the long sad stained planks of the floor lead-
ing to the back entrance which fronts Market Street where
the Greek coffee shops show dismal cardgames and *barbutte*
dice games going on in green interiors among gloomy men
in black, the long lost sad scenes.

"What you thinkin, Leo, will we do it before 8 o'clock?"
comes the cry now in English from the rhythmic chomping
press where inky Manuel (inky from so much) in blue
striped scullion's apron stands feeding sheets between the
yawns of inkpan and types, sheketak, sheketoom, shketak,
shketoom, and out come orange circulars advertising stores
their Spring bargains and Specials:——

THE MODERN WONDER

S h o e   S a l e

MEN'S SHOES	WOMEN'S	BOY'S SCOUT SHOES
$7 or $8 values	$6 low shoes	$2.49
As low as $2.98	Goodyear welt	
	$2.98	

THE MODERN SHOE STORE

143 Central St   Opp. Talbot's

——to be delivered door to door by boys on bikes or by Tao
hoboes who assemble under the pharting trills of birds at
daybreak to receive their day's bagful of circulars, which
will go for booze and beans——

"All I gotta do, Manuel, is finish this ad and get my foldin done, turn the key on Red Line Taxi and Cantwell optical, be done. Did you finish that new Pollard mat?"

"The great underpriced basement? All done, Leo, everything twenty-three skidoo and ready to roll."

"Well oil her up, we 'll be outa here by eight and maybe go down to the Keiths' for a game."

"Ah ben mué, les cartes, son pas assez bon pour la soif pour mué,(ah well me, cards, they're not good enough for thirst for me.")

"Ben mué too shpeux usez un bierre,(well me too I can use a beer,")both of them suddenly reverting to Frenchy slang since nobody's there to hear them anyway, just as you might expect the Greeks that you could see across the way thru the great dirty wire windows, breaking from their usual Greek to talk some English for the benefit of business there "ska ta la pa ta wa ya" here we go again, the great raving *patois* of Lowell on all sides, Polocks on Lakeview Avenue and Back Central, and practically pure Gaelic or at least lilting lyric Gaelic English on the Highlands and downtown——Syrians to boot, up the canal somewhere——And your old New England Yankees eating Indian Pudding for desert in old stately houses with lawns, on Andover, Pawtucket and Chelmsford, with names like Goldtwaithe and Smith——And thin noses and thin lips and read *Walden* by the fireplace on howling nights——

Eight o'clock Pa and Manuel close up shop and go across the street to the Jewel Theater for a chat with the manager Sam, the cameras are running off the latest photopaly replete with thrills and fast action and gray rain streaming across the screen and the piano rumbling suspense thunders in the pit, the oldtime movie stars with their prim painted lips set grim——"We grow through suffering," is written for what says the hero in flickery letters, "Jesus God," says a bum in the seat, "by now I oughta be as big as the side of the house" ——Sam gives them an introductory warming nip that goes like a prairie fire thru Manuel's belly, then they get back in the contraption and go bouncing down Merrimack to the Square, as acquaintances shout *"Weyo,* Emil, when you gonna enter in the races? Buy yourself some goggles and a hat that comes down over your ears! Manuel'll get you in the river, give im time!"——

"Ho Emil, how's the boy?"

"Ho Slattery——still swingin em?"

My father is a popular fellow around Lowell, in insurance he's buttonholed practically every small (and some big) businessman in town and extolled the virtues etc. etc. of seeing that your grave doth not rot in vain and you leave your successors some of your ghostly change——Then as a printer, to get ad-work, he'd followed up old acquaintances and hotfooted everywhere and was a proficient, nay much more proficient with the non French usually Irish segment of his customers, a proficient persuader and general good-time Charley——"Ha ha ha!" rang his harsh laugh, and you heard him cough as he left thru the door, bound for another——

They go rattletrapping in the strange comic French Movie contraption down past the City Hall and for want of shamelessness go sneaking thru the back streets to avoid the great Main Kearney Square where all Lowell's in the lights—— The clock, the Chinese restaurant, the Number One sodafountain, the trolley stops, the big stores, the newspaper—— They go instead around by Kirk street and down a railroad switch alley for the mills, across spectral-in-my-mind Bridge Street where stands the great gray warehouse of eternity and into the little alley that runs between it and the stagedoor side entrance of the B.F.Keiths theater.

"If you want your moonshine there he is now, old Henry ——I'll meet you backstage."

Emil goes under the iron fire escape and's just about to disappear inside when some of the vaudeville performers who have gathered in the warm night for a smoke, call him over——As one-time ad man making up the B.F.Keiths Vaudeville ads he is wellknown by a lot of the performers on the famous old circuit——

"If it aint Ben Oaklander, where's your piano, boy?"

"Emil——What you been doin these past two years—— know Billy here, Billy Dale?"

"*Shore* I know Billy Dale——Say, what's on tap with the new show?"

"Just opened tonight——There's Rialto and Lamont, the Talkless Boys——Oh, Lois Bennett, you know her——"

"A Ray of Western Sunshine——"

"——Western Sunshine, and Muriel Pollock the Popular Composer——and old Prop-Prop himself——"

"Prop-prop, did they ever throw him in the canal like they said they'd do the night he puked all over the trunks and suitcases?"——

"No——Say, boy, we took pity on him——Wal, you know what happened to him, wal, he's in South Bend now; wal sir Emil, how are you boy?"

"And do I understand we've got the dainty captivating vivacious Miss Corinne and Dick Himber offering Coquettish Fancies with Ben Oaklander on the piano?"——

"Say, boy, you got that memory——Yes sir, and there's Bob Yates and Evelyn Carsen in 'Getting Soaked' by Billy Dale and Bob Yates and there's Clarence Oliver, 'Wire Collect' "——

"I'll be damned, he's still around——"

"Yes sir, old mountain man too, and Billy McDermott the only survivor of Coxey's Army and on the screen a photoplay of speed and derring-do, me boy, forget what the name of it is——"

"A little bit of canned music, a title, a couple of sighs, and there's your money's worth——"

"Me boy, if it wasnt for vaudeville the man on the street wouldnt have a place in the world to get himself a good night of entertainment——Pathe News and topics, and Aesop's Fables all right, but when you got them flesh n blood performers up there, me boy, that exit march at eleven

P M wouldnt be worth the paper 't'scored on! Stop me if I'm lying."

Bend the drapes to your purpose——

And as they're standing there, smoke fragrantly rises from their cigarettes to the spring moon, and here crunching down the cindered alley comes a man in a strawhat (like Emil), but fatter, huge, with cane and great pot belly and bulbous red nose, a namelessly battered and muggled eaten-up and almost disappeared face:—— Old Bull Baloon.

"Emil, want ya to meet Bull Baloon here——"

"Glad ta meet ya——"

"This the boy plays poker?"

"Same."

"How 'bout a little swiggle a Mother Machree's ancient revitalizing monkey juice, Mister Emil?"

"Why——well——"

"Sometimes known as continental bug joy juice, or *joie de vivre*" (Old Baloon pronouncing it JWA-DAY-VIVRAY to Emil's great amused delight)——

"No, no, non, non, non——it's *joie de vivre,* I'm French, I know."

"This here business at hand, the poker game, somebody called Charley Sagely, and somebody O-BRIEN or other, brings my attention to the fact that——" upending his flask, swallowing, looking around, wiping the neck of it,

"——brings my attention——" but again repeating it slowly as now his eye has caught one of the principals coming down the alley and it's time to get the game underway, and meanwhile Manuel has come back with *his* bottle, and they all go inside to start the game in one of the dressing-rooms——

As the game progresses the participants increase, and soon they can hear the B.F.Keiths' orchestra playing the exit march in the pit and the audience is filing out for a soda in Paige's or Liggett's Drugstore or in Dana the Greek's and there will be dense dyed neon of oldtime city night in America, like old cartoons showing the boy newspaper seller with little cloth cap and scarf and knickers holding out a paper to two men, one in derby, one with elegant cane, their coats flapping in the aftertheater wind, and beyond, a great crowd, some reading papers, and the wallsides of buildings in the city night and the dimmed marquees and the general drizzle of activity in the furthest reaches of the scene, where I see Gerard's dead face—Old Fish Street, it is all incredibly dense, dark, soft, rich as if Spanish Night, the blue of tombs is in the neons, the secret of the Old Fish is on Old Fish Street, the dark spoor of real profound red throbs up from the assemblied lights and makes a halo overhead, it is all slightly alien, ugly, but soft and kindly——It is a dream, in the middle of it the kings and queens are being dealt by the mysterious cardplayers in the empty theater.

"What in the hell kinda concoction by the way you got in that new flask, Bull?"

And he, Old Bull Baloon, man of a long life (60) cluttered with a hundred thousand misadventures the whole story of which can never, will never be told except you see it written in the picotée carnation of his nose, the swim of winkles in his eyes, the wrinkles there, indicative of earlier olden eyes like of a hardboot on a Kentucky rail, the crooked coy smile and yellow-teeth, the big ring on thick Neroid finger like fingers of old whores successful and retired or fingers of Roman prelates given to regurgitation ere their excarnification comes due and all the banquets fall:——"It's a little mixture of wine, gin, and bourbon, I learned it in Panama some years ago with a little man named Low stood about four foot one inch and was half Chinese for all I know, lived in a wattle tenement on the edge of a river sewer system with dead rats and crapsticks floatin in the tide, and green spiders where he hid his dice——One afternoon some hobo from Pratt Street Baltimore I believe and I believe the name was Slats came up to Lady Nicotima at the bar and slapped her rump, congratulatin her for the good showing that afternoon, whereupon she turns around and says 'Dont you believe in God?' and aims a delicate little pistol and fires, hitting Charley Low dead between the shoulderblades and the bullet goes thru him and ends up I aint never seen him no more——and so," he says, receiving his hole card and his face card, "better be jocund with the fruitful grape, as sadden after none, or bitter fruit" (quoting Omar Khayyam) and glances down at his hole-card, a nine of spades.

"By God I dont drink as a rule like you do Bull——

Manuel you see this guy?"——to Manuel who's watching
the game sitting on a trunk drunk——"but by golly have
you seen that boy guzzle up that whisky tonight, Charley?
Jim? Two bottles now?"

"It's only two A M, give him a chance to start——"

"I've had to come from a long way and a lot of snowy
country to want that much heat, Emil."

"I'm *made* of water!" complains the stagehand who keeps
going to the toilet.

"Well, I like to gamble, like a drink once in a while," big
Emil glancing at his king of heart face-card and adjusting
it over the hole card, which now, surreptitiously, in the
middle of his sentence, he raises a corner of, to see the spade
smooth black of a 10 of spades, winking inside himself to
think, "but I never could drink like that and put it away
like that——hell George Daslin and me and Henry O'Hara
one time drink I dunno how much beer out of a barrel, in
Lawrence and then had whisky and a cardgame just like
this I guess 9 in the morning, whoo, it took ten years offa
my life——"

"I wouldnt tell you if I knew," says O'Brien now looking
at his hole-card with the same sly up-corner, saying to himself, so that the others can almost read it in the imprint of
the smoke before the lamp, "ten of diamonds."

Old Conductor Jim Sagely the railroad man, holding his
ace of clubs in one hand, thoughtfully raises the jack of same
underneath and purses his New England farmer lips.

"Sagely," says Bull, slyly, small blue eyes thru reddened

eyelid puffs watching, raising flask for a slug soon as he's finished his speech, a simp, "if I had a barrel a beans and I had a store, I'd hire you to count the bad ones and lay the good ones aside, that's how sly your dollar is."

"What are you, a Scotchman? A sneaky character you must be, with that false hat——bet it's got hinges on it. I aint no guy that lets his whisky bottle interfere with the waybills, or throws a switch and throws the crummy over before it's crossed the points."

"A lame, improfitable, infantile turn of talk if ever I heard one, your *crummies*——You? You're too miserly for *my* cardgame——it's midnight in *my* little life——what's *your* key?——Took 80 dollars from me last night——that represents a lotta claprous calls from the crew clerk and a lotta locals in the freezing air for an old Canadian National boomer like me."

"*Boomer? You?* You cahd shahp! Pool shahk!——First time I win some real money in my life and they's complainin in the sides and up the back——"

"**Le phantome de l'opéra,**" provides sepulchrally looking-over his shoulder, Manuel, looking to the eerie shrouds backstage deeper——

"Ne-mind the phantoms and drink your drink——You gave me a start, damn you!" says my father quietly chuckling.

"No complainin, Sage, I'm passin king of hearts Emil Pop here with his wife and kiddies just born, bang," throwing Emil a king of clubs face card, and everybody eying it.

"And Charles the hammer, bang, a queen of spades, two kings and two queens showing and where's the marital bed, bang, a jack of spades for the conductor, and bang"(for himself)"same of hearts."

"The game thickens."

"I bet and raise the ante."

"At this stage, nobody cares."

"And on this stage. A new ace wont do you no good—— old Sage could use it."

"Sevens——aint got no use for em, even when I got seven in the hole, my unlucky number, nine's my lucky number by God."

"Another seven——talkin of the devil——pair a kings high."

"There he is, Bull Baloon with a girl for his jack. Who's gonna win the rainbow pot?"

"Let me look and think." Emil, high, with pair of kings, pretends innocent worry. Charley O'Brien has nothing further to examine beyond his showing queens, but a mentioned forlorn seven.

"It's a dream, lads, it's a dream," utters Bull up-ending a lofty big pull on his swiggins, bloodshot returning the cap, spitting over his shoulder at the two spittoons in the corner. Sagely has a jack under and a jack on top, and nobody knows, but no advantage his, yet, till the last thrust of fate-cards, from the hands of the dealer, Bull. Emil leans over to rub his thigh in the night of the world forgetting his family, lost in the eye to eye the game of men in America;

nights long ago after Langford battered Johnson; smoke in Butte saloons; Denver backrooms, games; lost heroes of America; Chicago, Seattle; vaudeville redbrick alleys and forgotten cundoms under isolated signs in the highway night of Roadster Twenties; long jaws of bo's riding the boxcar from outside North Platte, to clear t'Ogallah, mispronounced, sad, spindle legged waiters in the summermoth night, by lights; America, sweaty, poker games, Negroes on the sidewalk in Baltimore, history, nostalgic with afternoon and man, midnight and weariness, dawn and O'Shea running to catch his train, Old Bull Baloon examining his useless King hole-card, half deciding to full decide to leave the game because even if he gets another King he's got no ace to ace-high Emil.

The others stay; Bull deals, lost in the dream. "Ten dont do you no good, Emilio, lessn you got another underneath," dealing Emil a ten of clubs. Deals Charley a seven, making a pair of 7's on the top. "You better have a queen underneath," which Charley doesnt have, stripped bare and queenless, turning up a 10 apologetically. "Another pair of Sevens!" dealing Sagely a 7 of hearts. "If he has another 7 underneath," opines the rednosed dealer from Butte Montana, "he's got his own deck a cards hidden in back of his ear inside that curly hair, yass. Which, would a left me with the Ace of Jokers," dealing himself, for the hell of it, the final fifth card tho he's out, the Ace of Spades, Death. "Gentlemen," seeing he's inadvertently emptied his flask without realizing it in the heat of what he was doing, "is there any beer in the house? No beer?"

"We got some left, yeh Bull, in the box there."

And Emil rakes in the pot, cigar in teeth, big body tensed forward in chair to affairs of the night, as goldpots strew the blue beginnings with incense of aurora and dawn creaks up to crack and boom over the black sad earth now irrevocably Gerard was, enfleshed, sacrificed and given over to, O moanin shame.

"I'm the one shoulda got that spade," comments Emil in the alley, as they urinate.

Bull, pointing up the dawn sky: "More ill fated than in all your dreams you'd a bitterly hoped her to be."

Then they get drunk——It happens all of a sudden, on the spur of nothing but a cry——"Slup a slug, son!"—— The high white mists of Spring morn over the redbrick roofs of downtown Lowell make them dizzily glad, they go (Manuel in the middle bawling) staggering down the alley——In two cars and the ridiculous motorcycle they go careering thru the mists and over the bridge.

"Where's that Irish club?——Where's that dog with the pipe in his mouth and the blue eyes who sits by the stove in the——"

"You mean Bob Donnelly, if he aint asleep now with his arms around his milky wife I'd bet and be damned and be called Tarzan if he wasnt still up and jawin his Jew's harp somewhere the other side a town——"

"And Murphy! Where are the river boys?"

"Never mind! It's a mystery!"

"Be Jesus Christ it makes me feel good, they lit the furnace in my damp cellar."

"All the blowers of hell'll send it thru the vents and veins and you'll come out with a true face at last."

They rave and scream as the wind ventilates them across the bridge, they're looking for the Polish Club that's supposed to open 24 hours a day, down on Lakeview——"That place with the chairs in front."

"Ah who needs a ga dam club——come down by the carnival grounds and piss in the bushes."

"Suits me fine, termagant."

"Manuel, what you doin, you almost got us to the end of our holes."

"They been swallowin a long time!"

"Then why not swallow more, lover."

"With my wife in hell everything suits me."

"You got eyes like a dead potatobug——wake up and watch the road!"

"Eat the damn road!" says Manuel who'd as soon the road ate him so they'd be where they were going sooner.

Irrelevent conversations meanwhile rage in the cars, driven respectively by Sagely and O'Brien, Old Bull Baloon in his red-eye cups now reconstructing adventures of six decades with the invention of sixty——They all spill out on the field at Lakeview Avenue, across from the mills, on the river, just as the blazing red sun kisses and peeps over the window roofs of all Centerville——

My father reels about from snort to snort, the earth morning under him——

My father with straw hat in big gnarled veiny hands, collar bursting out soft and unstylish over his coat lapels from folds of thick muscular neck, frown dark on his brow, hair curly, dark, crisp, nose bulbous, mouth grim but sentimental, kneeling on one knee, examining the sunrise with serious and exact and ponderous officialness, nodding slowly, "I'll tell ya Bull, there aint never been a mystery of this world I didnt stand in awe of, when standing in front of it, or kneelin on one knee as I am now." Strangely, rockily, the redness shows on the ridges of his face.

His head is held slightly on one side, as I say a little like Gerard, but in this case, the father's sadness is held inside a manly grace, or rather, a manly brace, the philosophicalness abides higher in the cranium here than it can in the recentness-film of the angel child——Experience has made a man of Emil, and you may take man and weigh him on the scales with his weight in goldshit on the other pan, the measurement may come out, legible——If so, write me a letter——I see no reason for Man——But his value, I buy ——Dawns white with drunkness I've had myself with my boys and after that were boys——And there'll be more—— Brothers that were saints that died on me, that too's happened a million times in a million repetitudes and reincarna-

tions in Samsara's sorrow parade——More wine! fewer dead potato bugs! Roll me down the road in a barrel, if I'm lying ——(and I've been rolled in a barrel down the road, an I'm a liar)——Jesus Child,——But birth and tender years which we take to be actual happeningness in the phenomena of this self belief that something seems to happen, called existence, hath made of Emil's son Gerard instead of a weighable debatable man, a tender-born and angel of tender years—— Emil's lips pressed together to make the whole face storm, Breton, hot, worried, Emil, leaning his big arms on thick unbreakable knees, thick thighs, he brushes the cigar smoke from the pants of his thigh, he fixes his face in the rising sun (priests are anointing and intoning a quartermile away), he looks like some Medieval wallguard waiting for the Jesus Child, nodding, "I'll be gol danged ... aint it a strange world, Bull——here we are, by the side of a river, two men—— once upon a time we had a notion we were romeos and gave up our little suspenders and our Saturday night nickelo-deons and made googoo eyes at the girls at basketball games and hit hero homeruns and then developed these big endless holes to thrown our money in——*money?* And all of it!—— Like throwing ten dollar bills and flowers in the gad dam ocean, Bull——"

"Expand upon the theme," says Bull passing the bottle.

"No I'm through—an ocean, Caesar never had it so good I'm tellin you."

Meaningless, they grow solemn and serious.

"It's a hell of a world——debts, wives, woman——scissors, meat, do you blame her?"

"Why hell no?"

"Ha?"

"Hell No!"

"In the winter, kiddies——a purple shame, an American shame, a durn Babe Ruth homerun of a shame——Youth gone wild, hung upsidedown——"

"Tarzan——"

"Emil, the world is happy!"

"You damn right."

"My best, MY children, I'm not promising anything——"

"End, but hole hat or no hole hat and happy sandholes of infantile or not, I predict it, seaweave breezes once in a while, sand most a the time, hot unhappy painful burning sand and right in his throat, and makes his wet yes water more"——(slup, a slug)——"Let the women wash it, I'm through, I'm the culprit officer, O offi sair, sir, but take me away not now, some other time Offi Sair Charley," as Emil and Charley dance and gesture Cop-and-Innocent Arrest on the red haunted banksides of 8 A M Lowell in the mud and molten snow——Harsh laughter, lighting of cigars, holding of them between fingers outstretched stiff drunk, the fragrance of the Cuban smoke, the Cuban quality of men, mixed with alcohol so many percent by volume and name your Infinity——Slapping of laugh-hands, Whoos!, and "Take me away peaceably, I wanta play one more game of poker!"——Pulling up of thigh pants, clearing of throats,

ah-hums and hem-haws, popping of eye-bulge doubts, star-
ings into the blank to wait for further time——

"O where's that Donnelly!"

"Well then goddamit let's go to him!"

Off they vow in their Immense vehicles——

"Oh call it a day!"

"And *why?*"

And when they do find Donnelly it's only for him to sit
there saying "Emil you could have ended up your days cryin
in that corner——calling for more drinks——but you had to
buy a store, and hire yourself out, and count your every
blarney."

"Aright with me, Ole Be-larney."

"And you hankered and pankled and popped to discover——"

"I did."

"And you——are you sure this is a mixture of what did you
say?" and later to the other old Irishmen of the corner, in
the store, the bloody store, he, Donnelly, says, "Emil Duluoz
——a perfect person," and they believe him.

But by that time we've all got big headaches——And our
Manuel-wives'll have a scream at us——And it's only stored
in bottles, tho you might think in furnaces of ire in Diablo
Bottoms——"The trouble with you, Duluoz," pronounces
Bull on our porch, the which even Gerard in his bed can
heart, at 10 A M——

"What?"

"You're just too eager to hear for me to tell you what's

wrong with you, so you can change and rectify——God made misers, and misers made God, and I'm suited."

They bump rolling heads together in the amazingness of this——

"Tst-tst," says my mother peeking from the kitchen, "it's looks like your father is drunk this morning"——"Who's that, that big pile? He's swallowed all his glasses and his barrels in his nose, it looks like!——They want some breakfast——I'll warm up last night's good *ragout d'boulette*" (pork meatball stew with onions and carrots and potatoes, exquisite, Old Bull Baloon never had a better meal since the time in Wyoming the fry-cook said to him at dawn "I got some nice homefrieds for ya this morning, Bull"——

O pitiful, lovable, soon-to-be-departed earth,——)
That'll do.

"And time bids be gone"——

It might be pepper for a cold feast, but I always did say that the fact that men *are,* is more interesting than anything they might do——'tis only a poor action on a part stage and the scenery (the fakery) can be seen to shift and jello, in the backdrops, the stagehands are clumsy, the designer clumsy, and thine eye quick——Inadequate settings, poorly paid carpenters——You wake up in the middle of the night and look at the horizon sneaking swiftly back into place, and you think 'O God, it's all the same thing'——That

there *is* a world, that, rather, there *seems* to be a world, is
hugely more interesting than what tiddly diddly well might
happen in it, like Nirvana in an ant-heap or an ant-heap in
Nirvana, *one*——

Bless my soul, death is the only decent subject, since it
marks the end of illusion and delusion——Death is the
other side of the same coin, we call now, Life——The
appearance of sweet Gerard's flower face, followed by its
disappearance, alas, only a contour-maker and shadow-se-
lector could prove it, that in all the perfect snow any such
person or thing ever did arrive say Yea and go away——
The whole world has no reality, it's only imaginary, and
what are we to do?——Nothing——*nothing——nothing.*
Pray to be kind, wait to be patient, try to be fine. No use
screamin. The Devil was a charming fool.

In his last days Gerard had little to do but lay in bed
and stare at the ceiling, and sometimes watch the cat. "Look
Ti Jean, the little nut——look, he looks one way, he looks
the other——Lookat the crazy face, what's he thinkin?——
Everytime he sees something what does he think?——Look,
he's goin in the other room. Why? What's he thinkin that
makes him go in the next room? Look, now he stops, he
looks——he licks himself——there, he yawns——well, now
he's comin back——he's crazy——O CRAZY KITIGI!
Bring him!" and I'd bring him the little grey tiger cat
and we'd biddle and fwiddle with his crazy nose and stroke
his head and he'd set in purring and glad. "Look at him, a
little crazy ball like that, a little white belly as soft and as

smooth as a heart——God made kitties I guess for us——
God sent his kitties everywhere——Take care of my kitigi
when I'm gone," he adds holding kitigi to his face and
almost crying.

"Where you goin?"

No answer.

"See? the little face, the little head, look, I could break
his head by squeezing my hand——it's only a little thing
with no strength——God put these little things on earth to
see if we want to hurt them——those who dont do it who
can, are for his Heaven——those who see they can hurt, and
do hurt, they're not for his Heaven——See?"

"*Oui.*"

"Always be careful not to hurt anyone——never get mad
if you can help it——I gave you a slap in the face the other
day but I didnt know it when I did it"——

(That'd been one of the last days when he felt good
enough to get up and play with his erector set, a gray
exciting morning for all-day work, gladly he'd at the breakfast crumb-swept newspapers of the table begun to raise his
first important girder when I importunately rushed up tho
gleefully to join in the watching but knocked the whole
thing over scattering screws and bolts all over and upsetting
the delicate traps, inadvertently and with that eternal per-
durable mistakenness we all know, he slapped my face
yelling "*Décolle donc!*" (Get away!) and must have instantly regretted it, no doubt that in a few minutes his
remorse was greater than my disappointed regret——) We

made up soon enough, head to head at the sad and final
mortal window, holy Gerard and I, which gave credence
now to his speech about kindness; and a speech it is, that
down thru the imaginary eternities, is, and hath been, handed
down by all spiritual heroes (of his like and calibre):——
immeasurable kindness——"It's in the words of the Lord's
Prayer——forgive us our sins, as we forgive those who sin
against us. Did you forgive me for hitting you?"

"Oui"——(tho I was too littly naive to know what it
meant *forgive,* and hadnt really forgiven him, holding back
that reserve of selfly splendor for future pomp)——As solid
as anything, as solid as the rock of the mountain, the solid
folly men and boys and women will have——"I hit you——
but I didnt have to, now I know it, the junk is packed away,
the thing I was building with my set" (he shrugs gallicly)
"I dont remember it any more!"

"The *grignot!*"

"Dont remind me," he smiles wanly.

"Ti Jean, dont bother Gerard, he's got to sleep this morning."

June, late June, with the trees having burdgeoned green
and golden and the beeswax bugs are high chickadeeing the
topmost trees embrowsying the drowsy air of reader's noon,
the backfences of Beaulieu street sleeping like lazy dogs,
the flies rubbing their miser forelegs on screens, "The little
flies too, you dont have to kill them——they rub their little
legs, they dont know how to do anything else——"

"Sleep Gerard, the doctor wants you to sleep——Go outside Ti Jean, you've talked enough this morning."

And I cry, to lose my buddy, whose pale door is closed
on me, and there he is with his protected little kitty in the
fold of his sheets and the birds are at the window waiting for
more of those familiar crumbs from his sure hands——

The doctor comes more often, leaves sooner.

I wander up and down Beaulieu Street, lonely, little, a
little Our Gang Rascal with no gang and no comedy and
no ring-eyed dog or Pancakes to throw——All alone in mid
afternoon I sit on the highwood backsteps of the St. Louis
Bazaar hall and strive to imitate the sound it makes when
Uncle Mike Duluoz and his wife and all the Duluozes drive
over from Nashua to visit us and sit in the parlor and lament
——"A BWA! A BWA!"——I'm especially imitating Uncle
Mike, the hurt curl of his lips——His great rouge cry-face,
poor Uncle Mike had he seen that, my little pantomime of
him, he'd a wept cruds to the earth to add to the woe——

"Cut out that noise, you little brat——we've been listening
to that bwa-bwa all morning!" shouts a woman from the
tenement washlines across the way——I cant go on with my
A-BWA play, go back to the house, Gerard's asleep, Ma's
doing the wash, I go in the cellar, it's dark and damp and
sad——My mother calls from the door above "Your little
chum is back!" meaning some child from down the street
I'd befriended a few weeks ago and now I dont remember
him from beans——Hands aback clasped I go to Gerard's

bedroom door, he meditates gently in mid afternoon, the shades drawn——

"Ti Jean," he calls me, "take my pillow and raise it a little——there——thanks——I wanta see my birds outside ——raise the shade——tick tzick tzick birdies!"——His breath smells like crushed flowers——I see and behold the sad sideways look for the last time, the long triste nun-like face, the blue eyes in their hollows.

Soon he's asleep on his sitting-up pillow.

When the little kitty is given his milk, I imitate Gerard and get down on my stomach and watch him greedily licking up his milk with pink tongue and chup chup jowls——

"You happy Ti Pou?——your nice *lala*"——

They see me in the parlor imitating Gerard with imaginary talks back and forth concerning lambs, kitties, clouds.

July comes, the pop firecrackers start coming on like a war in the neighborhood——Gerard's room takes on the quality of a lily, white, wan, fragrant——My mother and father are shaking their heads——

"What's the mater with Gerard?"

"He's very sick, Ti Pousse."

Ti Nin and I wait on the porch wondering what's wrong.

I wanta go in and talk to him but I'm not allowed—— The doctor turns up the sheets and looks at Gerard's swollen legs and says "That must hurt——I've never seen a kid like this——keep giving him that prescription——How you feelin Gerard?"

Gerard unaccustomed to being spoken to in English, answers, with girlish lips made so by sickness, or girlish-should-I-say-beautiful lips, "I'm aw-right, Doctor Simp-*kins*," with the accent on "kins," like my mother talks——

The big doctor betakes his black suited bulk out of that house of sorrows and goes home, having given up hope a long time ago——

Some time near the 4th of July he tells my mother to call the priest——"He cant have the strength to go any further" ("if he does," adding to think, "it'll be murder")——

My father, arms loaded with paper bags in which are firecrackers, with an expectant smile comes in that night, but he's told the priest will be called——With that comes the nuns, there they come down Beaulieu Street, three of them, to sit at Gerard's bedside praying——He's awake.

"How are you feeling, Gerard?"

"Awright, my sister."

"Are you afraid, sweetheart?"

"No my sister——The priest blessed me——"

They ask him questions which he answers briefly and softly, my mother sees the nun taking it down on paper—— She never saw the paper again——Some secret transmitted from mouth to heart, at the quiet hour, I have no idea where any such paper or record could have ended or could be found today, lest it's written on the rock in the mountains of gold in the country I cant reach——Or some fleecy mystery imparted, concerning the kinds of fearlessness, or the proof of faith, or the ethereality of pain, or the unreality of death (and life too), or the calm hand of God everywhere slowly benedicting——Whatever, the solemn tearful nuns did take it down, his last words, at deathside bed, and betook themselves back to the nunnery with it, and crossed themselves, and you can be sure there were special prayers that night——Saint Teresa, who promised to come back and shower the earth with roses after her death, shower ye with roses the secret nun who understands, make her pallet a better one than canopied of Kings'——Shower with roses and defend all the lambs and war the wraithful doves around ——I'm afraid to say what I really want to say.

I dont remember how Gerard died, but (in my memory, which is limited and mundane) here I am running pellmell out of the house about 4 o'clock in the afteernoon and down the sidewalk of Beaulieu Street yelling to my father whom I've seen coming around the corner woeful and slow with strawhat back and coat over arms in the summer heat, gleefully I'm yelling *"Gerard est mort!"* (Gerard is dead!) as tho it was some great event that would make a change that would make everything better, which it actually was, which granted it actually was.

But I thought it had something to do with some holy transformation that would make him greater and more Gerard like——He would reappear, following his "death," so huge and all powerful and renewed——The dizzy brain

of the four-year-old, with its visions and infold mysticisms
——I grabbed Pa and tugged his hand and glee'd to see
the expression of likewise gladness on his face, so when
he wearily just said "I know, Ti Pousse, I know" I had that
same feeling that I have today when I would rush and
tell people the good news that Nirvana, Heaven, Our Salvation is *Here* and *Now,* that gloomy reaction of theirs,
which I can only attribute to pitiful and so-to-be-loved
Ignorance of mortal brains.

"I know, my little wolf, I know," and sadly he drags
himself into the house as I dance after.

The undertakers presumably carry the little no-more-body
of no-more-pain-and swelled-legs away, in a tidy basket, to
prepare him for his lying-in-state in our front parlor, and
that night all the Duluozes do drive up from Nashua in
tragic blackflap cars and come to crying and jawing in the
brown kitchen of eternity as suddenly in my mind, as tho it
was only a dream, a vision in the mind, which it is, I see the
whole house and woe open up from within its every molecule
and become instead of contours of walls and ceilings and
absence-holes of doors and windows and there-yawps of
voices and lamentings and wherewillgo-beings of personality
and name, Aunt Clementine, Uncle Mike, cousins Roland
and Edgar, Aunt Marie, Pa and Ma and Nin at the lot, just
suddenly a great swarming mass of roe-like fiery white-

nesses, as if a curtain had opened, and innumerably revealed the scene behind the scene ("the scene behind the scene is always more interesting than the show," says J.R.Williams the *Out Our Way* cartoonist), shows itself compounded be, of emptiness, of pure light, of imagination, of mind, mind-only, madness, mental woe, the strivings of mind pain, the working-at-thinking which is all this imagined death & false life, phantasmal beings, phantoms finagling in the gloom, goopy poor figures haranguing and failing with lack-hands in a fallen-angel world of shadows and glore, the central entire essence of which is dazzling radiant blissful ecstasy unending, the unbelievable Truth that cracks open in my head like an oyster and I see it, the house disappears in her Swarm of Snow, Gerard is dead and the soul is dead and the world is dead and dead is dead.

I've since dreamed it a million times, down the corridors of Seeming eternity where there are a million mirrored figures sitting thus and each the same, the house on Beaulieu Street the night Gerard died and the assembled Duluozes wailing with green faces of death for fear of death in time, and Time's consumed it all already, it's a dream already a long time ended and they dont know it and I try to tell them, they wanta slap me in the kisser I'm so gleeful, they send me upstairs to bed——An old dream too I've had of me glooping, that night, in the parlor, by Gerard's coffin,

I dont see him in the coffin but he's there, his ghost, brown ghost, and I'm grown sick in my papers (my writing papers, my bloody 'literary career' ladies and gentlemen) and the whole reason why I ever wrote at all and drew breath to bite in vain with pen of ink, great gad with indefensible Usable pencil, because of Gerard, the idealism, Gerard the religious hero——*"Write in honor of his death"* (*Écrivez pour l'amour de son mort*) (as one would say, write for the love of God)——for by his pain, the birds were saved, and the cats and mice, and the poor relatives crying, and my mother losing all her teeth in the six terrible weeks prior to his death during which time she stayed up all night every night and grew such a mess of nerves in her stomach that her teeth began falling one by one, might sight funny to some hunters of conceit, but this wit has had it.

Lord bless it, an Ethereal Flower, I saw it all blossom—— they packed me to bed. They raved in the kitchen and had it their way.

There's the rocking chair, Uncle Mike's wife had it, the peculiar dreary voice she had, fast way she talked, things I cant utter but I'd roll and broil in butter, the gurgle in their throats——I could recount the dreary yellings and give you all the details——It's all in the same woods——It's all one flesh, and the pieces of it will come and go, alien hats and coats not to the contrary——Uncle Mike had a greenish face: he had barrelsful of pickles in Nashua, a sawdust oldtime store, meat-hacks and hung hams and baskets of produce on the sidewalk: fish in boxes, salted.——

Emil's brother,——"So *vain,* so full of ego, people——shut your mouth you" he finally says to his wife, "I'm talkin tonight——in the great silence of our father we'll find the reasons for our prides, our avarices, our dollars——It's better any way, now that he's dead his belly doesnt hurt any more and his heart and his legs, it's better"—— 1967- 1994 RIP K.C.

"Have it your way," says my father listlessly.

"Ah Emil Emil dont you remember when we were children and we slept together and Papa built his house with his own hands and all the times I helped you——we too we'll die, Emil, and when we're dead will there be someone, *one person* for the love of God, who'll be able to look at us in our coffins and say 'It's all over, the *marde,* the fret, the force, the strength'?——more's the strength in the belly than anywhere else——finished, bought, sold, washed, brought to the great heaven! Emil dont cry, dont be discouraged, your little boy is better——remember you well what Papa used to say in back of his stove——"

"With his bottle on Sunday mornings, aw sure that one was a smart one!" (the wife).

"Shut your mouth I said!——All men die——And when they die as child, even better——they're *pure* for heaven—— Emil, Emil,——poor young Emil, my little brother!"

They shake their heads violently the same way, thinking.

"Ah"——they bite their lips the same way, their bulgey eyes are on the floor.

"It ends like it ends"——

My mother's upstairs sobbing, lost all her control now——

The aunts are cleaning out the death bed, there's a great to do of sheets and an end to sheets, a Spring cleaning.

"I brought him on earth, in my womb, the Virgin Mary help me!——in my womb, with pain——I gave him his milk!——I took care of him——I stood at his bedside—— I bought him presents on Christmas, I made him little costumes Halloween——I'd make his nice oatmeal he loves so much in the mornings!——I'd listen to his little stories, I examined his little pictures he drew——I did everything in my power to make his little life contented——inside me, outside me, *and returned to the earth!*" wails my mother realizing the utter hopeless loss of life and death, the completely defeated conditionality and partiality of it, the pure mess it entails, yet people go on hoping and hoping——"I did everything," she sobs with handkerchief to face, in the bedroom, as the Bradleys, Aunt Pauline, her sister, come in, from New Hampshire, "and it didnt work——*he died anyhow*——They took him off to Heaven!——They didnt leave him with me!——Gerard, my little Gerard!"

"Calm yourself, poor Ange, you've suffered so."

"I havent suffered like he did, that's what *breaks* my heart!" and she yells that and they all know she really means it, she's had her fill of the injustice of it, a little lame boy dying without hope——"It's *that* that's tearing my heart out and breaking my head in two!"

"Ange, Ange, poor sensitive heart!" weeps gentle Au: Marie at her shoulder.

Nin and I are sobbing horribly in bed side by side to hear

these pitiful wracks of clack talk coming from our own human mother, the softness of her arms all gashed now in the steely proposition Death——

"I'll never be able to wipe that from my memory!"—— "Not as long as I live!"——"He died *without* a chance!"

"We all die——"

"Good, damn it, good!" she cries, and this sends chills thru all of us man and child and the house is One Woe this night.

Meanwhile, insancly, our cousins Edgar and Roland have sneaked off with the firecrackers to the backyard, and like leering devils, which they arent really, but as much as like satyrs and Mockers and be-striders of misfortune, there they are setting off all our precious firecrackers, Nin's and mine and Gerard's, at midnight, callously, a veritable burning of the books of the Duluozes, Ker plack, whack, c a ka ta r a k sht boom!

"*Les mauva, les mauva,*" (mean! mean!) Ti Nin and I scream in pillows——

The Bradleys are going to drive us to Nashua for the night and bring us back for the funeral in 48 hours—— With Gerard and the firecrackers all gone, and Ma crying on the very floor, we had better be driven somewhere——

When Ti Nin and I were little.

Then comes the solemn funeral, Nin and I are taken back on a rainy dreary day to see the house all one great Gloom Shrine full of kids from the St. Louis Parochial School filing in and out in frightened parades, their eyes straining to see the deadface in the unholy velvet pillow among the flowers, the sooner they see it the quicker they'll know the face of death and fears be justified all——And files of nuns, standing by the coffin, praying with long black wooden rosaries——All dolled up in little necktie I cant believe it's my own house and this, this World Parlor with Histories of Black being written in it, the very selfsame silly drowsy parlor where I'd sat and goofed away whole long afternoons chubbling with my lips or going goopy goopy at the window passers, or with Gerard (whose head I hold no claim on any more) held head-to-head confabs and listened to the holy lazy silence of Time as it washed and washed forever more——But now, his bier a glory, in death all Splendidified, banished-from-hair-earth and admitted-to-Perfectness he lies, commemorating our parlor silently, tho no one knows precisely what I know——But others know something of him I never knew, the nuns, and some of the boys, and mayhap Père Lalumière the *Curé* who now in the kitchen with one ecclesiastical blackshoe up on a chair and manly elbow on knee assured my mother "Ah well, be not anxious, Mrs. Duluoz, he was a little saint! He's certainly in Heaven!"

That was the reason for the big crowd, they came to see the little boy in the neighborhood who had died and gone

to heaven, and housewives even that day began noticing
and announcing that the flock of birds, the nation of phebes
and peewits and meek and lowly whatnots that had pes-
tered at his window for so long since Spring broke in, was
gone——

"They're gone completely."

"You dont see one."

"It's 'cause it's rainin!"

But the next day, and the next day, and the next day after
that, the little ones revisited no more the scene of the
deicide——

"They're gone with him!"

Or, I'd say, "It was himself."

Unforgettable the files of children come to see the cheek
they knew so well in classrooms, to see its loss of lustre
pink, and estimate the value of death——With what avid
and horrified eyes they gazed on little Schoolmate so re-
posy silent in his ornate bed——What horror even just to
approach the house and see the wreath, with the fatal pale
blue ribbon, and the fatal drawn shades in the parlor——
The vultures do feed on disconsolate such-rooftops when
you look, the chimney exudes angels of fear like whirligigs
of gray butterflies. . .

What you learn the first time you get drunk at sixteen,
tugging at old urinaters in Moody Street saloons and yell-

ing "Dont you realize you are God?" is what you learn
when you understand the meaning that's here before you
on this heavy earth: living but to die. . . look at the sky,
stars; look at the tomb, dead——In invoking the help,
Transcendental help from other spheres of this Imaginary
Blossom, invoke at least, by plea, for the learning of the
lesson:——help me understand that I am God——that it's
all God——Urinating, alone, wont get you far——It happens, every day, in all the latrines of Samsara——*Here and
Now,* said the children seeing *"Ti Gerard Duluoz qu'est
mort"*——"it's not any harder'n that——they wont be able
to punish me any more"——Beyond punishment, he lies,
qualified for eternity and perfectness——"Is it *true* he's
dead?——mebbe he's kidding"——and all the ghost feelings
of men——But no, "that bareheaded life under grass" is no
"blithe spirit"——It's the genuine death.

All the desperate praying in the stuffy parlor is scaring
the kids half to death, they think "It'll happen to me too but
look how they're all afraid of it?"

Clasped in Gerard's kindly fingers is a beautiful solid
silver crucifix——There are flowers from relatives in Maine
who couldnt come, from friends——All the people in the
world who wear their daily face come passing with their
final face, as, for instance, Manuel, sober, dark-attired, un-
accostably silent, he wont even speak to the priest, to Emil
he makes one regretful nod——He'll be one of the pallbearers.

Old Bull Baloon is gone west, wont be at the funeral.

The women, the aunts, stand at the back and are never weary of shaking their heads from side to side, and *lamenting the loss,* and talking about it——

Young priests make polite calls and add their powerful prayers and depart swiftly to duties in the gloom——One of them has such a handsome sad face, it's a shame he never married and presented it to some respectful wench——

"The young Lafontaine!"

"Aw oui——he comes from Montreal——I didnt know he was so short."

"Yes but he's so pretty."

"Pretty? Handsome as a heart——It's too bad——All the good men are bought up or else won."

"One or the other."

"Look here comes old lady Picard——she never misses one——"

"No——Oh well, the old lady, we'll accept her prayers."

"Her prayers are not to be thrown away."

"There——the little angels——another line——This one, they tell me it was Gerard's class——yes——the nuns are puttin em in front——there. The little angels. They're afraid."

"Ah"——sigh——"they'll have to know *some* day, it happens to all of us."

"Ah, but he was so young."

"Look at that old bat across the street, she's burning her garbage and all the smoke blowin on the house of the dead with the wind."

The house of the dead indeed, it was hardly my house——
I'd lost Gerard in the shuffle.

High above, in the stormy sky, a bird with little buffeted
birdy bones bats ahead, beak to the nose of the wind——
Shrouds of gray rain fall Awe-ing and slanting to our crystal
——It is the sky, the void, that no fist could form in and
hold any part of it——Below, on the stain of earth, where
we all, human brothers and sisters, pop like flower after
flower from the fecund same joke of unstymied pregnant
earth and raise standardbearers of fertility and ego-personal-
ity, life, below the blown shrodes and woe-bo blackclouds
June is handing down from some whoreson unseasonal
storm, patches of brown and yellow and black show where
we live, chimneys are pouring black smoke——"The Chim-
bleys of the World!"——And we are angels revisiting it
——Coming down, far, sad, wide, the world, the earth, this
pot, this place, this parturience-organizer——There are the
chimney smokes fuming up and pouring and defiling open
space, and there the tracks, cracks, cities, dead cats floating in
rivers, calendars on the wall indicating June 1926——License
plates on old cars sayin Massachusetts, the helm and Chinee-
mark of it——The name of a store, in gold leaf letters
embossed and chipping already, "Lowell Provision Company," a self-believing butcher with a handlebar mustache
standing in the door, full of human hope and realistic sen-

timentality among the charnels and hacked thighs of his own making, bleedied in his blocks, his hands raw from blood-juice, red in fact——Shakespeare, Throwspeare, Disappear Spear, and where is the Provision made for a "cessation and a truce" to all this sprouting of being just so it can wilt and be sacked, canned——We the angel spirits, descend to this earth, earth indeed, we are awed to see living beings, living beings indeed, we see man there ghostly crystal apparition juggling as he goes in selfmade streets inside Mind a liquid phantom glur-ing on the brain ectoplasm——A vision in water——

Papier-mâché canals flow in downtown Lowell, men smoking cigars stand by the rail spitting in the waters that reflect drizzle hopelessness of 1926——And to their way of thinking, ahem, the money in their pocket is real and the pride in their heads as real as sin and as solid as Hell—— And the money that is real and the pride that is solid is about to buy an actual porkchop which tho it has since appeared (it is now 1956, Jan.16, Midnight), the hunger with it, and the hungerer to boot, can still be called *real,* tho it neither *is not,* nor *is,* but beyond such considerations anyway, like a reflection of a porkchop on water——Facts well known by fat Mr. Groscorp who now, in his apartment across the street from the St. Louis Presbytère, on West Sixth Street, is about to partake of his noonday meal at the kitchen table by the rain drizzled window that looks down on the street where suddenly a slow caravanseri of limousines and flower-roadsters has rounded the corner from

Beaulieu Street, and headed up to the church front, where official waiters minister with the proper silver special knobs ——His face is huge, muckchop rich as kincobs, sleek as surah, gray pale and fetid to-make-you-sick, a great beast, with small mouth makes an oo of simpery delight, and great hanging jowls——A bathrobe, slippers, a fat cat—— Winebottle and chops laid out——His huge paunch keeps him well away from his fork, and makes it necessary for the eating-chair to be scraped a good deal of the way back, so that he stoops, or rather hunches forward with huge mountainous determination, like a tunnel, to his about-to-be-eaten lunch——"Ah," he interrupted, "another corpse!" ——And he raises napkin to lips, and watches leaning up to see below closer——"In all this rain, they're gonna bury another one,——aw dammit, it's a pity, it spoils all my meal ——It all goes down the same hole, why make such a great ceremonial fuss?——The solemnity, the gloves——the special gloves and the stiff legs——the little mousey smile—— the little mustache——the big hunger for nothing to eat, or else the great famine in the richness of the season——One or t'other, it's all the same, because," raising his eyes to the upper part of the window and examining the blown gust clouds, "you might say"——he burps delicately, lowering the shade——"That, there's plenty more where it came from, the comin and the goin——Outa my way, I'm eating—— We'll think about it later——"

The funeral directors with their cars had assembled at our door on Beaulieu and carefully, from our great drear house built on an old cemetery in which were more dead soul dusts than in all the words of this book, its sorrow was removed from its nest——Sleek like a snake the coffin was slid out and in the hearse, bang.

And around the corner.

The children and some onlookers follow on the sidewalk, the church is only a block and a half away.

Right by the building where huge Mr. Groscorp's eating his necessitous Samsara dinner, is a gang of painters and plasterers and tile layers working on a new house—— They've just had their last lunch slug of coffee and feel good and make cracks.

"Ah, another one for the cemetery?"

"Why dont they hurry up, damn them, it's not so much fun playin with the dead in the rain!"

"An old bastard who fell face first dead in his soup, I bet."

"Or else some old bitch spent all her life yellin at her husband and her brother, now they wont hear her no more ——Do you believe those hypocrite faces you see?"

"Or else an old priest, dead in his bed."

"Or else an old housepainter, he fell off the ladder and spent six months in the hospital yelling 'A dammit it hurts!' and after that they carried him out."

"No——too gay——a whore, from Boston, returned home, she spent sixteen years in the whorehouse swingin her ass for a buck and now the funeral director with the little ass's got half, and——"

"And the rest lost in the bank a the dead."

"Throw em some rice, we'll marry em!"

"Look, they stopped to take out the coffin."

"Coffin for the so-pretty" (*Tombeau pour les si beaux*).

"It's not a long one——"

"It's not a long one?——dammit, it's a child's coffin."

They all get quiet.

"Ah, well that's a story we forgot."

"We're not good enough storytellers."

"Well me I'm paintin."

"Paint, dog, till your hand close your buttons."

"Till they put a brush in your mug, my fine Piroux, and after that we'll sing dirty songs for ya."

"Suits me."

"Look——that little coffin, the kid wasnt ten."

"All the better for him."

"And why?"

"*And why* he asks me with his ignorant face?"

"It's raining on your head, come on in here."

"There'll be plenty of rainin on the head today."

And inside the church now as the procession comes in, the pallbearers carrying the little coffin, followed by Ma and Pa and me and Nin and relatives, across the gritty sidewalk, great comes the opening peals of the organ sounding the beginning of the mass.

"Suscipe, sancte Pater, omnipotens aeterne Deus, hanc im-
maculatam hostiam, quam ego indignus famulus tuus offero
tibi, Deo meo vivo et vero, pro innumerabilibus peccatis, et
offensionibus, et negligentiis meis, et pro omnibus cricum-
stantibus, sed et pro omnibus fidelibus christianis vivis atque
defunctis: ut mihi et illis proficiat ad salutem in vitam
aeternam. Amen."

An eternal salute. . .

One of the first if not the very first, memories of my
life, I'm in a shoe repair store and there are shelves cluttered with dark shoes, innumerable battered shoes, and it's
a gray rainy day (like the day of the funeral, or rather,
foggy-misty with occasional drizzle)——I'm presumably
with Ma and probably one year old in my baby carriage
(if it happened at all) and the Vision is of the great Gloom
of the earth and the great Clutter of human life and the
great Drizzly Dream of the dreary eternities, and as we
leave the shop, or, as is left the shop, by self or phantom,
suddenly is seen a little old man, or ordinary man, in a
strangely slanted gray hat, in coat, presumably, walking off
up the dreary and endless boulevard of the drizzle dump,
the tearful beatness of the scene and weird as if maybe this
is just a memory of mine from some previous incarnation
in St. Petersburg Russia or maybe the gluey ghees of dark
fitful kitchens in Thibet ancient and long ago, tho not with
that hat——That hat, with its strange Dostoevskyan slant,
belongs to the West, this side of this hairball, earth——And
it seems to me that the little man is going towards some

inexpressibly beautiful opening in the rain where it will
be all open-sky and radiant, but I will never go there, as
I'm being wheeled another way in my present vehicle——
He, on foot, heads for the pure land——So that it seemed
to me as the organ music played and the priest intoned in
Latin at the altar far up the pews in the end of time, that
Gerard, now motionless in the central presented bier at
the foot of the main aisle and by the altar rail, with his long
face composed, honorably mounted and all beflowered and
anointed, was delivered to that Pure Land where I could
never go or at least not for a long time——Dread drizzle
mer, dread drizzle *mer!*

"Et pro omnibus" sings the priest in rising and falling
Latin, incense everywhere, and turns with that untouchable
delicacy of lace over holy black, with all his paraphernalias,
and it seems in my 3-year'd brain "et pro om-ni-boos" is
the description of that land and that attainment, the glory
of Gerard——(that was prophesied)——*"aeternam,"* the
gloomy fall of the song voice, "eternity," I can almost guess
and smell the location and no way in my wild mind to
muddle my way and shake off——And I'm so little and so
far back, and in my reveries and dreams later on it seems
the funeral took place across the street from our house in a
strange other church permeating everywhere——Just as the
simplest thing in the world, when properly looked at, is the
original riddle.

——Way at the back of the church are blankfaced standers, it's like Good Friday when the church is crowded and

it's usually raining (and according to superstition) and there are standers at the back in overshoes or rubbers or with umbrellas who want to quit swiftly the snowy grace and get back to the poolhall——I dont understand anything of the funeral service, its solemnity escapes my high head as I look around and mull over faces of people and those tragic overshoes and wet splashes of almost puddles at the back of the church and the hopeless dampness as tho it was all taking place underneath some stone steps and there are the drear shadows making the yellowy marble so faint, so sad ——The daubing at eyes by aunts and mothers, their faces squeezing into sections wishing he hadnt died, ah, seems to me fitting and proper, it's all part of the show——It's a vast ethereal movie, I'm an extra and Gerard is the hero and God is directing it from Heaven——

I see bleak wooden fences in the rain and the little man with the mysterious hat and then my mind swirls and I see nothing but the swarm of angels in the church in the form of sudden myriad illuminated snowflakes of ecstasy——I scoff to think that anybody should cry——I let go a little yell, my mother grabs my face and taps me gently, *"Non non non"*——People gloomy at the funeral have heard the little child's voice, they think: "He doesnt understand."——

I want to express somehow, *"Here* and *Now* I see the ecstasy," the divine and perfect ecstasy, reward without end, it has come, has been always with us, the formalities of the tomb are ignorant irrelevencies most befittingly gravely conducted by proper qualified doers and actors and Latinsingers——Of a rouse, the boys' choir takes up in the back and my mother's eyes burst with tears, she never could stand boys singing anyway.

"Some of them knew Gerard!" she announces proudly to near-at-hand solemn Emil and thru him at Marie—— "The little angels!" ("Sing, sing," she thinks, "sing with all your hearts my angels for my friend Gerard who is dead, my little man, my little sad son——It's for yourselves you sing, angels!!")

I myself hear the boys singing and turn around to see them in the choir loft with their little oo-voices uplifted and rosy to the black arms of a hypnotist, a hypnotist of feeling——By the way the boys are singing and by significant rustles you can tell the service (and increasing coughs) is almost over——Easy enough to cough cough cough and go back home, off other people's funerals!

And Oh the coffin at the forefront, and the priest flicking the ciborium incense pot and at each flick, in three directions, by some magic bell rope signal, the outside roofbell flicks like smoke itself and kicks off a soft "ker plang" for the edification of the people of Centreville, Gerard has died ——Drizzly news——From the incense pot, 'ker-tling,' so gentle and quiet, to the sound of the connecting signal rope, 'kak,' and 'ker plang,' such beautiful music and I see three fumes of music smoke float up and away——Let there be rejoicing.

We all get in cars and they slowly weave the parade and out we go on a long slow drive along the Merrimac River,

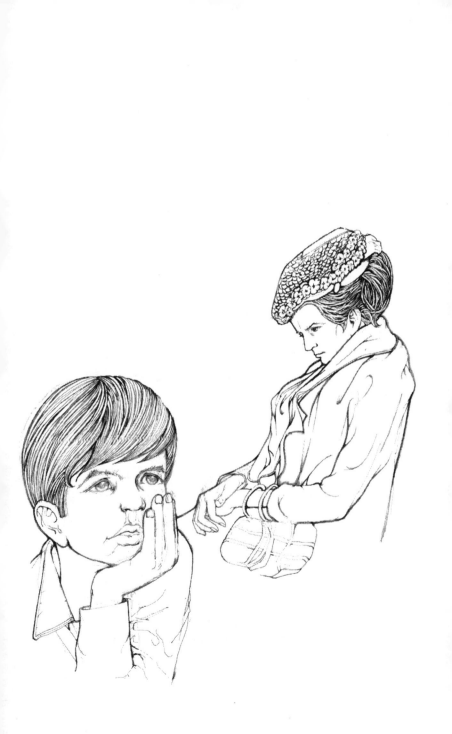

by sodden trees in all their foliage looking sad, to the bridge at Tyngsboro, and across that, to Nashua, entering that little city (my parents' come-from town) in bleak array, to the cemetery outside town, where I remember the long gray wall, and the glistening boulevard in the rain——And they haul the coffin gently down to graveropes that for all their gentle look have no gentle job to do, and lower away, easy does it, the little hunk of pain, into the mud——Roots and plopping pieces show in the dug sides——Men stand around, my father in the midst of them, bareheaded, with that gooply helplessness beneath immense and endless skies that say "Yah" down upon the entire scene——My father's curly hair is moist, and uncombed, and his lids of eyes are down where they'll always be——A cold place to kneel, this earth, and he'll kneel again, it's a cold place for knees—Ma and Ti Nin sitting with me in a black car burst out sobbing as the coffin downward disappears, I turn to them and say "Well why are you crying?"

"Ti Jean you dont understand, you're too young to understand!" they wail, seeing my rosy face, my questioning eyes.

I look again, the men have stepped a pace aback, expectant, old gravedigger picks up his shovel and closes the book.

T H E   E N D

Sometime in the same
night that's everywhere
the same right now
and forevermore
    amen